# GORGONS DESERVE NICE THINGS

# ALSO BY TANSY RAYNER ROBERTS

# GORGONS DESERVE NICE THINGS

TANSY RAYNER ROBERTS

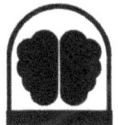

Brain Jar Press
PO Box 6687
Upper Mt Gravatt, QLD, 4122
Australia
www.BrainJarPress.com

Cover design by Peter Ball
Cover Image: *Antique Silver Medusa*, 80's Child/Shutterstock; *Animal Background Rug Texture*, Carpetpatterndesigner/Shutterstock; Antique Signs and Symbols, oxygen_8/Shutterstock.

ISBN: 978-1-922479-37-2 (Ebook) | 978-1-922479-38-9 (Chapbook)

# CONTENTS

# MEET ME AT THE MEDUSA

We all have snakes for hair.

Some conceal them below wigs and hats. Some stay inside, never venturing out to be seen, and judged, in public. Some wear them proudly, spilling over crisp white collars and leather jackets.

Did you see Ann Veronica in *Vogue* last week? Designer sunglasses blocking out the light, and serpents trailing down her shoulders over the very latest boho silk sheath cape. She looked a million dollars. She looked exactly like she didn't care that her hair was hissing at the camera.

I have never felt so represented.

I have never felt so scared.

There was a time, not so long ago, when none of us could be seen in public. We met at the Medusa, a private club for ladies like us (and not like us). There and only there could we be free to let our snakes fall where they might; though we still covered our eyes with sunglasses as a matter of public safety.

I turned the first man I ever loved to stone. At the Medusa, surrounded by my people, I know that every single one of them has a similar story.

We are not alone. We are not monsters.

We all have snakes for hair, and we deserve nice things.

~ど~

We all have snakes for hair. And yes, that does not only mean upon our heads. Shaving is not an option; waxing can be done with discretion and a delicate touch. But we don't all have the budget for a private beautician, or even to visit a salon that caters to monsters like us.

At the Medusa, in one of the back rooms of the bar, Amelia comes twice a week to service our needs.

Every tiny snake pulled from its roots survives, under her care. I once stood on the balcony at the back of the club, looking over the yard as she released them, one by one, into the wild.

~ど~

Ada is the concierge at the Medusa. She's not one of my kind — not a *gorgon* (yes, I whisper the word if I must say it at all, I still remember the centuries when they came after us with swords). Membership of the Medusa is open to a wide variety of monsters, each more gorgeous and dangerous and secretive than the next.

I don't know what Ada is, but I know I want to be her when I grow up.

Ada can get you anything you need. If you're a member, she has your back. Whether it's a tank full of spiders to eat, an inconvenient corpse to disappear, or tickets to *Hamilton*, Ada can make it happen.

I once saw her face down a dragon, eight-foot high, in the Periwinkle Tea Room on the third floor. The dragon went from wanting to burn the whole place to the ground, to sobbing on Ada's shoulder about how her girlfriend dumped her for a harpy.

I ran into Ada once, outside the club. She was standing in a queue for a taxi, looking sad and grim. In the daylight, her complexion is not the flawless china surface that it appears to be inside the walls of the Medusa.

People were staring. As I got closer, my snakes concealed beneath an over-sized beret, I stared too. I couldn't help it. She had shapes writhing beneath the paleness of her skin. Tentacles, I realised, as I looked closer. Dark shadows of the sea. And scales, not dragon scales, but something altogether more... sinister.

I caught her eye as my path crossed hers, brave enough to offer a friendly smile. I'm trying to be better about these things.

Ada smiled back, held her hand out to me as I passed by, and we exchanged a discreet fist bump.

Not all snakes are literal.

~〰~

The monthly meeting of the Snakes for Hair Book Club is held in the Peacock Parlour, on the second floor of the Medusa. A closed session, gorgons only, so that we can let our hair down both literally and figuratively as we read Ovid in translation, Christina Rossetti, Theodora Goss.

A naga recently applied for membership, on the grounds that she feels she is snake enough to join us as we discuss the fierce works of our favourite writers: Mary Shelley, Octavia Butler, Jeanette Ng.

It does not feel comfortable to exclude her, and yet, and yet.

(We have not yet made a resolution about her application.)

~〰~

Membership of the Medusa does not require an annual subscription — and thank goodness for that, or most of us would be priced out of its beautiful, antique rooms. As it is, I barely have the budget to pay for my own drinks, one weekend a month.

You must be sponsored by an existing member to join. And of course, you must disclose your nature to the President, currently a sleek mermaid who holds her meetings in the large subterranean indoor pool, three floors beneath ground level.

On the day I arrived, thirty-four years old and shaking in my boots, I was guided to the pool by my sponsor, Madame Marie, who chose to mentor me when I first arrived at the laboratory with my new by-correspondence biology degree.

'Trust her and tell the truth,' Madame M said at the pool's edge, removing my sunglasses from my eyes and putting them on top of her own head, which writhed and hissed.

I removed my clothes, my boots, my layers of disguise. Naked, with snakes that fell from my scalp past my shoulders, I stepped into the pool.

The water writhed and bubbled. There were creatures in here with us, dark and shadowed. One of them brushed my leg. I did not scream. Who was I to judge?

The mermaid emerged from the water, hair slicked back, breasts bare. Scales covered her from her hairline all the way down. She met my gaze with her own, and she did not turn to stone.

'Why do you want to be a member of the Medusa Club?' she asked.

I could have said many things. Of how much I had heard of the club and its discreet facilities. That I wanted to be a scientist, and so many of my heroes were members here.

Instead, I went with simplicity. 'I want to be with my kind. I want to learn how to take pride in being a monster. I deserve this.'

The mermaid smiled. 'Welcome to the Medusa,' she said, and reached out her scaled fingers to stroke my snakes, like a grandmother tidying me before a public appearance. 'You will find friends here. A little luxury. Comfort and kindness. Also, we have an excellent therapist on retainer.'

Snakes for hair.

Sometimes it's a metaphor.

Sometimes it's not.

Sometimes it's a cocktail: *Snakes for Hair* is my favourite listing on the drinks menu in the Banshee Bar, all Kahlua and vodka and mint chip ice cream.

Sometimes it's a way of life.

Sometimes it's a secret password.

Sometimes... it's the truest thing anyone has ever said to me.

Meet me at the Medusa one day soon. I'll buy you a drink and show you around. If we deserve nice things, then you do, too.

# HOW TO SURVIVE AN EPIC JOURNEY

Fill my cup with wine, girl. Pass the honey cakes, and I shall tell you a tale of adventure and heroes. I was there. I knew them all.

~𝓛~

## (1)

Meleager liked to think it was for his sake that I ran away from home and joined the crew of the *Argo*. Ours, he believed, was the kind of epic love that bards sing about from one age to the next.

He even believed this sober.

I loved him well enough, but I had no illusions about how our song would end. He had a wife at home, for all he pretended otherwise.

No matter. With Meleager warming my side at night, the rest of the crew kept their hands to themselves, and I was able to make the most of the adventure I stole for myself.

I signed my name to that enterprise for love, yes, but not love of a man. I fell in love with a ship: the *Argo*, a beautiful lady in the hands of a captain who never deserved her.

Jason is remembered as a hero, and I do not dispute that. But I think perhaps the definition of the word 'hero' has shifted over the years.

We all know men like Jason. He was tall and muscled and golden: it was easy to believe he was favoured of the gods.

The gods have shit taste when it comes to picking favourites.

I should have known there was something wrong with him from the first — you can tell a man's worth by how he treats his servants. Our Jason was busy flogging an oarsman when Meleager first led me to the dock at Iolcus.

Young and thirsty for adventure, I ignored the warning signs. By the time I had the full measure of Jason as a captain and as a man, I had already fallen for the *Argo*: hook, line and sinker. I would have put up with any amount of bullshit to be part of her maiden voyage.

Jason ruined everything for his crew: the quest, the prize, even the legend that followed. We hoped to do great deeds, and be remembered as...

Yes, all right, I'll say it. Heroes.

Instead we ended up as supporting characters in Jason's tragic romance with himself. Sometimes, we are not even that. I myself am often cast out of the Argonaut legend because the idea that Jason might have allowed a woman on board a ship is beyond the pale. (Hesiod, I'm looking at you.)

Everything that Jason did, all those stories testifying to his selfishness and excess, and you fucking poets think risking a maid's virginity is where he might have drawn a moral line?

I am Atalanta of Arcadia, and I was there. My life map allowed two possible roles: to be a spinster princess or a married princess. I chose a third.

I chose to be an Argonaut.

## (2)

I did not care a wet fart about the Golden Fleece. To sail and to fight, to be a comrade alongside my fellow adventurers, was all I ever wanted. The Fleece was an excuse, a story to sail ourselves into: it could as easily have been a monster to slay, a crown to collect, or a stable to scrub clean.

It was Jason who believed that the treasure gave us purpose.

As the *Argo* neared Colchis, we rescued four sailors from a wreck and they asked us whither we were bound. We told them, and they were surprised.

'You know the king of Colchis is an eccentric host,' said one.

'He claims to be son of Helios,' said another, with a smirk that suggested he did not believe the tale. 'And he punishes those who challenge that claim.'

'You're not mocking the gods, are you?' my shipmate Perseus demanded. He was one of at least three sons of Zeus on the voyage, not including Herakles who had abandoned us weeks earlier.

'Nay, friend, but when a king wears a golden hat with spikes and regularly descends into his throne room on a string and pulley so as to pretend he is the sun itself....'

We all agreed that it would be hard to keep a straight face with such antics going on.

'My crew and I are on a quest to steal the Golden Fleece so that I can reclaim my father's throne,' Jason declared proudly.

The four sailors stared at him a long while and then, in unison, laughed so hard they were nearly sick.

This did not bode well for our quest.

## (3)

Jason claimed that Herakles jumped ship in pursuit of a lover. We knew better than to believe our captain's lies by then.

There had been blazing rows between the two heroes, and not only when they were in their cups. Herakles believed a hero should do more than collect shiny trinkets and kiss up to royalty. (This was rich, frankly, coming from him.)

Jason, as royalty himself, took those insults personally, and insulted Herakles in turn for his treatment of women. (I know. Believe me. The hypocrisy did not go unnoted.)

A crew cannot survive with two captains. We owed Jason our loyalty even if most of us agreed that Herakles would make a better leader.

So Herakles left and the boy Iolaus scurried after him.

The *Argo* was lighter and quieter with them gone. No one argued with Jason for a while, and the next time we slew a sea monster, we toasted the name of our good friend, Herakles the hero.

He met a bad end, of course, but not before Jason met his.

## (4)

Let me tell you about this hero of ours, captain of the beautiful *Argo* (seriously, that ship was spectacular, it breaks my heart the way she ended).

On the isle of Lemnos, Jason seduced the local queen, only to abandon her with a thickened waistline. I don't mean that he baked her a nice cake before we stole out in the dead of night without paying for a winter's worth of bed and board. I mean he knocked her up.

It was a terrible winter. Our mast cracked in two places, and there's only so much you can do to repair wind damage to sails before there's nothing left of them at all.

Thus we arrived on Lemnos: the isle of women, surrounded by a stormy sea. All their men had left, in boats that never returned.

While Jason negotiated for us to winter on Lemnos, our heroic Argonauts joked that it was the women's hairy legs, or their smell, that sent their men packing. This was a fishing island, and I can tell you now that the smell of fish scale and bone had nothing to do with the women.

We could have been happy there, Meleager and I. We learned to fish, and it was easy enough to forget about my lover's own abandoned bride while we were so far from home. But adventure called, spring awoke, and thanks to Jason's honeyed promises to the queen (who still believed they would marry before her babe was born) we had to slide the *Argo* into the water under cover of darkness and make away in secret.

Jason laughed that night about his narrow escape, and I seethed at him in silence. For love of the *Argo* and the quest ahead of us, I said nothing.

No hero ever claimed to be a good person.

## (5)

Let me explain more about Jason.

You would think he had been born to the crown, that his childhood was all pomp and silk cushions and 'your Majesty' and sweetmeats, every inch of wealth and privilege ever extended to a child. A life like the one I ran away from, as fast and far as I could.

In truth, Jason was raised far from all that. The son of a usurped king, he was hidden as a baby, raised by peasants or by centaurs, depending on which story you believe.

My money is on centaurs. There was nothing humble about our Jason: he was all piss and arrogance. Every step he took was in the expectation of an embroidered carpet sliding beneath his foot. No peasant-raised creature would ever behave thus.

When he came of age, Jason presented himself to the kingdom of Iolcus in Thessaly to claim his father's throne, armed with fairy stories and a sharp sword. This was inconvenient for everyone, not least his uncle Pelias who was enjoying the job of king.

Jason had lost a sandal on his journey while helping an old woman (possibly the goddess Hera) across a river. Clytius of Troy reckoned it was more likely Jason lost the sandal while shagging a wine maiden. You can guess for yourself which version sounds more authentic to my ear.

An oracle had warned King Pelias he would be killed by a man with one shoe, so he was never going to embrace his nephew in friendship. Destiny and paranoia collided.

'What would you do, dear boy, if a man came before you whom the oracles had foretold would be your murderer?' the wicked uncle asked Jason over a cup of wine.

Jason, never the quickest ship in the fleet, wiped wine off his mouth and said 'Give him an impossible task that will see him killed; or at the least, out of your hair for a year or three.'

How they laughed.

The next day, Jason was sent on his epic voyage to claim the Golden Fleece and prove his worth.

Would I have joined the crew if I knew our quest was deemed impossible long before I even reached Thessaly? Hells yes. I would have fought a dragon for a chance to fly the *Argo* across the waves. I would fight a dragon for that ship still, if she was prepared to wait a little longer for me to lay my old-lady cane down and ready myself.

If she still sailed; the *Argo* never got a chance to become a crone like me.

Putting up with Jason was a price worth paying, or so I thought back then. I had no idea how steep the price would rise.

## (6)

So, there we were in the waters of Colchis, finally. We arrived, tired and hungry, presenting ourselves as friendly travellers seeking royal hospitality from a dangerous king. Our mission: to steal his most precious and beloved treasure.

I know what you're thinking right now. You're thinking, 'What is the worst possible thing Jason could have done to sabotage this difficult and sensitive task?'

How exactly did Jason of Thessaly fuck it up?

I present the following evidence: The King of Colchis had a daughter. A young, barely marriageable and voluntarily chaste daughter.

The epic poem writes itself, doesn't it?

Medea reminded me of myself. She was a princess who would rather be anywhere than her father's palace. She wanted to escape, and in Jason she saw a handsome, golden prince straight out of a children's tale. She saw a hero.

She was smart, Medea, but young, and she crumbled beneath the golden boy's charm. She became our secret weapon — we would never have got past the dragon or escaped the city without her.

Later, years later, Jason claimed that Medea's love for him was a gift from the gods; if that is true, then he is not the only one in debt to Aphrodite.

I would be dead, were it not for our quiet, dark-eyed princess and her skills of healing. Medea saved me.

If only she could have saved herself.

# (7)

The worst part of that night...

I can't speak of it yet, give me a moment to gird my strength.

We ran, Argonauts all, back to our ship with the stolen Fleece and the stolen princess. There were shouts and cries and torches, and we knew how badly we had gone astray.

King Aëetes was going to kill and eat us all, and who could blame him?

Two hard-faced young warriors with fine clothes and expensive swords — Medea's brothers — met us at the dock, ready to kill us all. My Meleager and Perseus and the others stepped up to fight at Jason's side.

I was already hurt, having taken the kind of slow wound you don't recover from, while our fearless leader was seducing his new girl.

Our heroic crew made short work of the princes and left them bleeding out on the ground. We had to step over the bodies to make the ship ready: ropes and sails flying through our hands.

I dragged the Fleece aboard, wretched and foul-smelling thing that it was.

Medea stood on the docks, wrapped in her shawl. Jason hovered on the gangplank of the *Argo*, his hand outstretched and faltering. Did she want to join us or not?

'We should bring the bodies,' she said finally. 'My father is a superstitious man. If we separate their limbs and scatter them in the seas, our pursuers will be delayed by trying to restore the bodies of the princes.'

We all stared at her. What a mind she had, to come up with such a plan: devious and devastating.

'Make haste!' Jason cried, hauling Medea aboard. He gave the orders to seize the bodies and bring them on deck.

It was foul work that we did, butchering those corpses and

dropping the pieces one by one in the waters of the shallow shores of the Aegean.

True to Medea's prediction, the men of Colchis collected our grisly gift, piece by piece, and risked drowning to plunge after the pieces that floated further and further away.

We sailed to safety.

'A strange people,' Jason said later, his eyes on the princess as she worked on my belly, smearing the neatly stitched wound with a poultice that stung my eyes with its fumes. I would not die after all. Her hands were cool as she worked; her face professional.

Medea had served Hekate since she was six years old. Her skills went beyond a talent for potions and creams. She was witch, sorceress, priestess. She was more dangerous than anyone on our ship.

Jason saw only a girl that he wished to possess.

I lay back on the ship's deck, in a haze of sweet-smelling drugs and the smell of my own blood, while Medea saved my life. Through my heavy eyelids, I observed the princess, that angry, powerful, dead-inside witch, and I thought: *that girl needs a friend*.

## (8)

Never let Meleager tell you the story of the golden apples, especially when he's drunk.

It is not his story to tell.

The story of the apples belonged to a younger, prettier man: Hippomenes of Thebes. Hippomenes Fleet-Foot. Hippomenes Sharp-Wits.

I had already run away from home once by the time I was sixteen. I joined the great Hunt for the Calydonian Boar, a monster set upon the world by a vengeful Artemis. This was my first taste of what it was to be a hero: the Hunt was full of men desperate to earn a line or two for themselves in an epic ballad.

Men, and me.

King Oeneus of Calydon called for heroes to save his kingdom from the rampaging beast; he forgot to specify that those heroes be male. When I arrived with my bow and leathers, many so-called adventurers refused to join the hunt if a woman came along. Meleager, son of King Oeneus, was in charge of listing our names, and he thought it a grand old joke to let me play.

It was less of a joke when my arrow found the Boar first: fourteen of us brought the creature down in the final battle, but I had made first touch and thus, when the spoils were divided, I won the hide.

Meleager placed it around my shoulders and winked at me; I lifted my chin and thought myself dignified because I did not let him charm me into his bed. (Not then, at least, not yet.)

My furious father dragged me home to Arcadia. He demanded I marry like a proper princess, or dedicate my chastity to the gods — anything but live the life of adventure I had barely begun to taste.

Over-confident with the smell of fresh-killed boar hide still lingering in my hair, I pledged to my father this: I would marry any prince who bested me in a foot-race.

No prince was that fast.

I saw off dozens of suitors, all embarrassed and limping by the end of their travails, but it was Hippomenes who got the better of me.

This is the story that Meleager tells (that all men tell, when they repeat it): Hippomenes tossed golden apples before me as we ran, and thinking myself unbeatable, I allowed myself to be distracted by the pretty trinkets.

A princess after all: soft and weak for beautiful objects, for the gifts of the gods.

In truth: he did not throw apples, but rocks. There was no godly work in this. He broke my leg.

I never saw my father so furious as when he exiled Hippomenes from the kingdom; never saw him so guilt-ridden, so completely on my side.

So I asked a boon of him: to let me have my quest, as all heroes do, before they settle down. I almost had him convinced.

But my father could not imagine a world in which a woman was a hero without being raped and ruined. He refused me.

Once my leg healed good and straight, I stole myself all over again. This time, my father did not catch me. I found Meleager, and Jason, and the *Argo*.

Atalanta of Arcadia sailed into adventure, and never looked back.

## (9)

Ours was no grand romance. Meleager and I simply fell in with each other. I liked his wit; he liked the swing of my hips and my bold talk.

He thought himself in love; I did not challenge the notion.

If Meleager were not married already, I might have given in to the notion of being a wife: I liked the idea of a husband who could be friend and travel companion. His hands were warm and clever in the dead of night, while our friends slept around us on the deck. A future together would have been amiable.

But he was not free, and I was no Medea; there would be no poisoning of my lover's wife.

(That horror was still in her future, as the *Argo* creaked around us, carrying us home.)

Medea made a good companion. She charmed the men with cheerful prophecies of their noble futures. She made a herbal soup that made us all merry and filled our bellies with cheer.

As my mortal wound healed, I watched Medea blossom into the role of Jason's wife. Happiness suited her.

We faced monsters on the way back to Thessaly. Medea hypnotised them, and made them bleed. We grew comfortable and lazy as her powers steered us safely home.

She was heavily pregnant by the time we stepped ashore in the city where it all started. Pregnancy did not slow her down in the least; her fierce loyalty meant that she was already calculating how best to support her man.

There was a parade in Iolcus for the returned prince: Jason was given the people's ovation. He waved the Golden Fleece with one hand and clutched his stolen princess with the other. We followed in his wake, his Argonauts, waiting for the pomp to end so we could escape.

He had promised his ship to us. He would need the *Argo* no longer, when he replaced his uncle as king. We stayed for every feast and celebration, while King Pelias grew harder of face and stiffer of shoulder.

Meleager danced with me, wine on his breath and hands warm on my hips. 'We're not getting that ship,' he whispered, and I saw that his eyes were not as glassy as I had believed. 'We have to leave, tonight.'

'But he promised us the *Argo*,' I replied in my own furious whisper.

'Jason's going to need her to escape with his life,' Meleager whispered back. 'Look at them all.'

Above the celebrations, King Pelias and his daughters watched a would-be usurper dance his way across their banquet hall.

I loved the *Argo*, but I wasn't stupid enough to die for her. 'You're right,' I conceded. 'We don't want to be here for what happens next.'

## (10)

Here is what happened to Meleager: after many adventures: animals hunted, monsters slain, treasures found, he begged his lover Atalanta to return home with him and be his mistress while he filled his wife with a new generation of royal babies.

Atalanta refused politely, and they parted on good terms.

Meleager died many years later, in a fire that may or may not have been a curse from the gods. His family line continued. He had allowed his daughter to learn the bow and the knife; a better choice on whole than when he arranged for his sister Deineira to marry Herakles.

Heroes make the worst husbands.

What of Atalanta?

I took my own share of the spoils we won together and went

to Argus, builder of the original *Argo*, and one of our former shipmates. I commissioned a ship: the *Calydonian Boar*. She was a splendid craft, small enough to manage with a minimal crew.

I sailed into adventure.

Sometimes, I heard word of the Argonauts: of Herakles and his labors; of Laertes, father of Odysseus, of Perseus and Castor and Deucalion and all the rest.

The stories of Jason and Medea were the worst: they left murder and misery in their wake. King Pelias' daughters became convinced that Medea's herbs and spells were enough to heal their father of his silver hair and the pains of age, when in fact the best choice for his health would have been to give up the throne and live in comfortable retirement.

Medea's spells went wrong; Pelias died. The anger of the people sent Jason and his witch wife into exile. They went to Corinth, I heard. Corinth, a bright and prosperous city which had need of a new king, as long as he did not mind setting Medea aside to marry a nubile young princess.

Jason, you will be shocked to learn, did not mind that in the least.

## (11)

Long after the fellowship of the *Argo* ended, there were times when I missed Medea. It might seem strange to you, that I liked the woman; she was clearly a monster. And yet, there were many who thought the same of me.

We lived in a world that did not allow women to breathe; how could we be anything but monsters?

Medea saved my life. She sang songs that made the wind catch the sails faster. Her soup was delicious. I could use a witch like her on my crew, were she not busy with her children and her errant failure of a husband.

Years passed, and I did not hear from her. I hoped she had found happiness.

I had my own happiness: wind in my hair, wood firm under my feet, salt in my teeth. I had a crew willing to take orders from a female captain as long as I paid them well and looked the other way when they spent my gold on whores and wine.

One day, I received a letter that broke my heart. It said: *My children are dead, and Corinth wants me dead too.*

I went to rescue Medea. Of course I did. That's what friends do.

Jason's new bride Creusa was murdered. The method was a poisoned dress: a wedding 'gift' to the woman who stole Medea's husband. The people of Corinth hounded Medea out of the city. They hurled stones at her that did not find their mark, because she had doused herself in hasty protection spells.

The stones rebounded on her children.

Now she was alone and heart-sick, a prisoner of her own grief.

She was a monster, they said, for of course the city claimed that she had killed the children herself, in vengeance against Jason.

'I did not expect you to come,' she said when I broke open the lock on her prison door. 'I do not deserve to survive this, Atalanta.'

'Suffer if you must,' I told her calmly. 'But don't do it here. I have need of a witch on my crew. The pay is decent, and you will be far from that ass you once called husband.'

Medea frowned at me, as if she did not quite understand. 'They failed to kill me. I thought you might do it. You were always the noble one, of that whole crew. Your arrows fly the straightest.'

I rolled my eyes at her. 'If you must die, do it battling a monster or facing down an endless whirlpool of terror, like a normal person.'

'Like a hero,' Medea scoffed.

I took her hand, and led her out into the sunshine. 'If Jason counts as a hero, anyone can.'

## (12)

This is the story of the *Argo*, and how she died.

Of all Jason's failings, this is the worst: he let his ship rot. She could have survived for generations if he took proper care of her, but without children to carry on his blood, Jason grew bitter and more selfish.

He lived out his later years deep in his cups, allowing the greatest ship of our age to fall to wrack and ruin.

We grew old too, Medea and I; past the age of motherhood, we settled for being sailors and adventurers. The *Calydonian Boar* wintered on Circe's island every year, so that Medea could learn from her aunt, the greatest sorceress who ever lived. It helped, I think. Circe gave Medea a peace she had never known, the forgiveness of her last surviving family member, and the companionship of a woman who knew how to read and write and think deep thoughts.

I spent those winters wandering the island during the day, gambolling with sheep and goats, and reading epic poetry. In the evenings, we drank wine, ate cake, and told stories of our adventures to entertain our hostess. Sometimes a boat would deliver supplies from the mainland: honey, oil, spices, and the snippets of news and gossip that Circe was always keen to pay for.

I had heard about Meleager's own untimely demise exactly like this, three winters earlier.

Now Medea read aloud to us by candlelight. 'Jason's dead,' was all she said and then: 'Oh, the *Argo*,' as if her heart was breaking.

I have never loved her more.

Circe snatched the parchment from her niece. 'Her mast was rotted through,' she said in disapproval. 'That sounds highly unsafe.'

'Clearly,' said Medea. 'As it fell on Jason's head.'

We drank wine and shared a moment of silence for the ship that Medea and I had both loved so very much. Our first taste of freedom and adventure. We would always be Argonauts.

'If Jason is dead,' I said a moment later.

'It changes nothing,' said Medea instantly. 'We should sail the *Boar* further south this summer, if you're willing? I've always wanted to find a dragon.'

I grinned back at her. 'When have you ever known me to say no to an adventure?'

We sailed south; we found a dragon. But my wine cup is empty. Let that be a story for another night.

# GIRLS WHO READ AUSTEN

All Scylla wanted from a college roommate was someone who wasn't too messy or too tidy. Maybe, if she was really lucky, she might get someone she could hang out with on a weekend watching the 1995 BBC mini-series of *Pride and Prejudice*.

Instead, she got Charybdis: a dark hole of sadness who cried over her high school boyfriend every night, and wrote furious texts to him all day, threatening his current girlfriend, and faking her own pregnancy.

Scylla made friends that year: cool people who loved literature as much as she did. They'd spend hours in the coffee shop with her talking about Mary Shelley and Shakespeare and who would win in a knife fight between Mary Shelley and Shakespeare.

But all her friends were sorted for roommates, so she went back into the lottery in sophomore year and hoped for the best.

Aello didn't seem too bad at first, for a harpy. She didn't shower much, and she smuggled several illegal bird cages into their room, filling it with the sound of chirps at all hours of the night, and the smell of dry seed and stale bird shit. But she was an English major, at least, and she only brought her hookups home on weekends, texting ahead so Scylla knew to spend all night in the library.

Aello's friends, on the other hand, were total dirtbags. They smoked pot in the room constantly, stole Scylla's phone chargers, and made loud comments about how reading books at college was a waste of time.

So yeah, it wasn't the best year.

~~~

Circe, in junior year, was a breath of fresh air. She was beautiful and witty. Sure, she was a bio major, but she read novels for fun which automatically made her Scylla's favourite roommate so far.

After a few tentative conversations about period drama and favourite Austen adaptations, it emerged that they both had bigger crushes on Emma Thompson in *Sense and Sensibility* than they'd ever had on Colin Firth in *Pride and Prejudice* and then, well...

Circe's mouth tasted like honey, and she liked to play loud angry rock music when they made out on each other's beds. Their relationship escalated to grinding at parties, open-air kissing on every campus lawn, and on more than one occasion, public sex in the library.

Scylla almost failed out of her classes that year, at first because she was so wrapped up in her first proper romance, and then because of the fallout after she caught Circe doing both coke and her TA in their shared bathroom.

Second semester was hell, thanks to Scylla's ongoing resentment, Circe's refusal to admit she had done anything wrong, and occasional screaming meltdowns when the tensions pulled too tight.

~~~

'My hopes are not high,' Scylla told her senior year roommate, who lay on the twin bed nearest the window, watching lazily from behind mirrored sunglasses while Scylla dragged in her suitcase and her three cartons of books. 'I don't need us to be friends. I just want to get through this year, pass my classes, and graduate without any drama.'

Her roommate yawned, and her hair hissed. She reached down to a cage of mice beside her bed, selected one, and fed it to one of the snakes that was coiled on her scalp instead of hair. 'Sure,' she said. 'No drama. I feel you. But do you have a copy of *Northanger Abbey* I can borrow? My sister stole mine over the summer.'

Scylla stared thoughtfully at her. 'It's Medusa, right? Uh. You turn people into stone?'

Medusa clicked her tongue. 'That was one time, and he totally deserved it. Mostly, I read.'

Scylla unpacked her books slowly on to the shelves, leaving two free for Medusa just in case she needed them. When she was done, she sat on her bed. 'Sometimes I turn into a monster,' she admitted.

Medusa cackled. 'Time of the month, am I right?'

'No, I mean I actually, you know. Grow six heads. And extra teeth. My skin goes all grey and scaly and I want to eat people all the time. It can last for days, or weeks. I guess that's why, well.' She didn't know how to say *the administration gives me such crappy roommates* without being rude. 'They always pair me with other monsters,' she admitted finally.

Medusa lifted herself up on one elbow. 'Are you calling me a monster?' The snakes on her head rose up like a cloud of vengeance, their beady eyes all fastened on Scylla.

'No,' Scylla gasped. 'I didn't … just wanted to, you know, give you a head's up. About me.'

'Okay.' Medusa shrugged and flopped back down on her bedspread. 'Sometimes my boyfriend bursts into my room and tries to behead me with a sword. It's kind of our thing. So you know. Consider yourself warned.'

They lay on their beds in silence for a while, getting used to each other's presence.

'So,' said Medusa, a little while later. 'Did you hear they're doing another *Pride and Prejudice* movie?'

'This one better not have zombies in it,' Scylla muttered.

'Worse. Werewolves.'

'No! What the hell? I mean, maybe if it was *Mansfield Park*.'

'I know, right? I hear Jonny Lee Miller is producing because he wants to be Darcy.'

'When will that man leave Jane Austen alone? She's suffered enough.'

They laughed together, and Scylla let herself hope.

# THE LOVE LETTERS OF SWANS

The papyrus was warm between my fingers as I sat on the wall above the port of Sparta, feet swinging in the sunshine. 'She imports this from Egypt,' I said aloud. 'My mistress loves the Phoenicians and their magics. I believe she would gild the whole Palace if the king would let her.'

Chloris, sitting beside me, reached out a hand as if longing to touch the letter for herself, then let it fall. 'Your mistress is a slut, Hymnia,' she said. 'Everyone knows it.'

No, not that, never that. I shook my head at her. 'She's never done this before. Never made eyes at a single dignitary, or flashed her breasts at a passing prince. She chose the king good and proper, and she seemed to like him well enough.'

'And look at her now, making eyes at a Trojan,' said Chloris. Her eyes gleamed in the sunshine. 'Can I read this one?'

'Only if you know the secrets of the Nile,' I scoffed. 'My mistress is not going to let her words out into the world without enchantments on them, is she?'

'I know a few secrets,' said Chloris, reaching her hand out for the letter.

I held back, not wanting to let her try. 'There's a word that unlocks it. She gave it to me. But I mustn't tell you, it's only for his ears.'

The boat was not yet here, still bobbing out at the horizon.

'Tell me the word,' begged Chloris. She was so pretty, and so bold. I would never catch the eye as she did, nor command others to my will. Gods pity me, but I craved her friendship. She was a slave, every bit as I was, and yet I wanted her to like me.

'Eggshell,' I said in a whisper, and the papyrus shimmered before us. My mistress' words danced across the rough brown surface, burning like the sun.

~ゐ~

*Paris, Prince of Troy*

*Your words are attractive, and your poetry extremely elegant. I am impressed that you take so many words to convey a simple message: 'Fuck me, lady, I have earned you.'*

*Believe me when I tell you that nothing you or your goddess of love have ever done has earned a night in my bed, much less the disruption of my rather comfortable life.*

*You are a beautiful, shameless man, and you dishonour us both with your passions and your promises. Our poets run wild with tales of wives who lost everything because they believed a lovely, wicked tongue.*

*Do not write again, baby prince. You are out of your league.*

*Helen, Queen of Sparta.*

~ゐ~

'See?' I said, delighted. 'She's not a slut. She's sending him back where he came from, good and proper.'

'She's not virtuous neither, not with words like that,' said Chloris, much impressed with *fuck me, lady* sprawling across the page in gilded ink.

'He's hardly acting like a gentleman himself,' I sniffed. 'Begging her to run away with him, just because she smiled once or twice in his direction at her husband's banquet. Not a brain in his head, that one.'

'I'd give him a tumble in a heartbeat,' said Chloris with a throaty laugh. 'Half a heartbeat, all painted and oiled as he was that night, ready for action. He wore sapphires in his own ears. Imagine what he'd give to a wench he liked.' She shivered in delight at the thought of it.

I rolled my eyes and risked a friendly elbow in her direction. 'He had no eyes for any but my mistress. You think he'd want you? He believes the goddess of love has Queen Helen marked out for him, that she is a grand reward for his mighty deeds. He's not going to take a wine pourer instead.'

Chloris gave me a dirty look. 'There's more than wine pouring in my future. You just watch me.'

Queen Helen was bathing when I returned to her, the papyrus all but on fire between my guilty fingers. She reclined in a shallow bath as two house-slaves scraped at her skin with oil and strigils. Another combed and trimmed her hair close to her head, so that it would be comfortable beneath her many golden wigs.

Helen had learned many tricks from Egypt in her youth, when she and King Menelaos were first married and the world loved them for it.

She had secrets too, my mistress. Two long, fine scars ran down her back, between the shoulder blades and all the way to her waist, where the wings had been severed only days after her birth. My mother was midwife to Queen Leda, and always scoffed at the idea that Helen and her sister were born from eggs.

'That lady worked as hard as any other mother, to bring her screaming scraps into the world,' she insisted when anyone got a cup of wine into her.

No one wanted to know that, though. They wanted to know if it was true that the Queen had lain with Zeus in the form of a swan. If you've ever wondered how stories like that get started, you need look no further than the slaves after dark, drinking and telling tales of their masters.

'I'll say nothing more,' my mother would insist, and then if a cup or three were forthcoming, she would tell the tale of the baby princess who was born with white wings, and had to have them removed by a doctor's knife.

I always thought she was exaggerating, until I came to the Queen's household myself and saw those scars of hers. Occasional fine white feathers grew back along the scars from time to time, and discreet slaves plucked them out before they became too obvious.

Those scars weren't the only mark of the swan upon Queen Helen. White downy feathers grew thickly at her pubis, instead of curly hair, but she refused to let the slaves do anything about that. Menelaos, the king her husband, liked to be reminded that she was divine.

In bed, he called her 'my goddess' and 'queen of the heavens'. Hard to imagine she would look elsewhere, with a husband who saw the stars every time he gazed upon her.

Today, though, I was not sure her thoughts were on her husband at all. The queen tipped her head back, allowing Eurynia to massage her scalp with oils.

'What did the ridiculous prince think of my letter, Hymnia?' she asked in a lazy voice.

I hesitated. I had never spoken anything but the truth to my mistress, but today the truth might earn me a beating. 'He laughed, my lady,' I confessed.

'Did he indeed?' Helen sounded intrigued rather than angry. 'Did he scribble anything in return? A grovelling apology for his cheek?'

'He wrote you a message,' I murmured, trying not to think about how Chloris and I had already pored over his reply before returning to the palace. I was worried she would see it in my eyes, that I had betrayed her confidence to impress a friend. 'I have the papyrus here. The release word is "sea-foam".'

~ॐ~

*Helen, Queen of My Heart*
   *Your crudeness wounds me, though it makes you no less lovely in my eyes. Indeed, I have earned you. Indeed, I will fuck you. I offer*

*you my father's city across the wide waters, and myself — a husband young enough to keep you wet with pleasure for the rest of your life.*

*The goddess Aphrodite has spoken, that you shall be mine. I would bow down and worship you in her name. Helen will be wife of Paris, and princess of Troy. There is no other possible future for us.*

*You were made for our goddess, born of the lusts of Zeus and his concubine Leda. Your mother may have thought herself a queen in her own land, but she learned quickly that it is wise to kneel down in submission when offered a mightier phallus.*

*Submit to me, Helen. Let me love you. The seas will burn with the flame of our lusts, and the goddess shall be sated at last when you cry my name to the winds.*

*Paris, Servant of Desire.*

'Gods above,' Queen Helen whispered as the papyrus grew taut in her hands. 'This man is dangerous. There shall be no more letters, Hymnia.'

'As you say, my queen,' I said in relief.

Helen stood up, allowing the water and oil to cascade off her as she strode carelessly across the room, dripping on the mosaic tiles. 'No, wait. I shall write once more. I must convince him that I am an impossible mark for this quest of his.'

My heart sank. A bold young man like Prince Paris would surely respond to words like 'impossible' as nothing more than a challenge. 'As you say, my queen.'

*Paris, Prince of Fools*

*Queens and wives have been ruined for far less than these letters between us. We shall not speak, nor write again. You have nothing to offer me, younger son of a lesser land. I am the queen of the city that birthed me. I chose my husband to rule at my side. You will not break me nor tempt me to leave Sparta, and you shall never possess me.*

*Sail back to Troy and be grateful that you escaped the flames that would set the world alight if Menelaos, King of Sparta, thought himself cuckolded by a whelp like you.*

*Favourite of Aphrodite, never forget that I am a daughter of swan-shaped Zeus. Approach me again, and I shall peck your eyes out.*

*Helen, always of Sparta.*

We sat on the sun-kissed wall, Chloris and I, reading the letter that Helen had dictated, crossed out, and re-written more than a dozen times before she was satisfied with it.

'That's that, then,' I said, wanting to believe it. 'We'll never see him again.'

'Are you blind?' said Chloris. 'She's practically begging him to snatch her out from under her husband's nose. That's a call to arms, that is, not a farewell.'

'She wouldn't,' I insisted. Above all things, I believed in my mistress's fidelity.

'You'd better hope he sees it as a love challenge and not a rejection,' said Chloris.

My confusion must have shown on my face.

'Well, if he takes it as an insult, he'll lash out at you, won't he?' she pressed. 'Whip you, I wouldn't be surprised. Got no reason to be kind, if the lady he wants is having none of him.'

I had been whipped before, but not since coming into service for her mistress. Queen Helen had always been gentle in her admonishments when a mistake was made. 'He wouldn't dare, not the Queen's messenger,' I whispered.

'You won't be the Queen's messenger anymore, not if he don't need you to send no more messages,' taunted Chloris. 'And she can't defend you, can she? Not and risk him telling the king what the letters were all about. Best to drop the papyrus into the ocean, never let him see it.'

I drew my knees up to my chin and hugged them close. 'Can't do that. She'd expect the papyrus back.' One way or another, I could be in for a beating today.

'Tell you what,' said Chloris, with a smile as bright as day. 'I'll take it for you. I'm not afraid of the prince. And he won't know me, so can't risk offending my master, can he?'

I felt a shameful flood of relief. She was my friend after all. Maybe all this had been worth it. 'Really? You'd do that for me?'

'Why not? I fancy another glimpse of the pretty prince.' Chloris hopped off the wall. 'I'll bring the papyrus back after.'

~ઈ~

I waited on the wall as long as I could, but Chloris did not return. Finally, I ran back to the palace to perform my various duties. There was a fancy dinner on this evening and it was easy to keep out of the queen's way, with all the dressing and primping and tasting to be done.

I didn't see Chloris later, not anywhere around, even after the dinner started and most of the palace slaves gathered around the kitchen to share gossip about our guests.

Prince Paris had not made an appearance at the dinner, and King Menelaos took this as a grave insult, though Queen Helen did her best to smooth things over with him with her usual deference and humour.

I was sick with fear that the Queen would call me over to whisper privately about the return of the papyrus, and ask if there was some final missive from the bold, foolish prince.

So I busied myself at the feast, making sure there were others around me at all times so there was no chance the Queen could summon me. Not without making it far too obvious that she had a secret.

Later, as the feast settled in, I ran to the door slaves to ask if Chloris had returned to the palace. Both claimed to have seen her, which worried me. Why would she hide from me unless something had gone wrong? I hurried off to my nook in the chattel quarters and relief exploded in my chest when I saw the papyrus tucked into my sleeping roll.

If I was quick, I would be able to take it to the queen's rooms and leave it near her bed, so it would appear to her as if it had been there all evening. The previous word, 'honey pears', did not release any words. Either the magical papyrus was blank now, or the Prince had added his own lock upon the page. In any case, it should be safe from prying eyes.

I hurried along the brightly painted corridor that led to the queen's quarters, so engaged in my task that I barely heard the pot that broke, moments before I burst through the doorway.

And there, oh. A sight I wish I had never seen.

Queen Helen of Troy lay on her back in bed, sprawled beneath the flexing, sweaty muscles of a man who should not be here. Paris of the painted eyebrows and jewelled ears. Tangled together, they groaned and gasped with something that sounded more like laughter than passion.

Shocked beyond all reason, I pressed myself into the side of the door, hoping not to be seen.

Too late. Paris arched his back and looked at me over his shoulder, poised to thrust again into my mistress. 'Like what you see, little one?' he snorted.

Helen gave him a shove so that he fell, wet from her and still hard of phallus, back on to the bed. 'She's no use,' she protested, swinging a long leg over to straddle him like he was one of those horse gods the Trojans favoured, taking him deep inside her. 'Little Hymnia is good as gold, and would never summon anyone to see her mistress's terrible secret. Break another pot.'

There was something in the way she said those words, a mocking tone that I had never heard in the mouth of the Queen. Still, it was familiar. My embarrassment overwhelmed me, red and hot, and yet I let my eyes fall downwards to the place where flesh met flesh. Coarse hair curled around her mound, hair that ought to be feathers. The creature fucking Prince Paris in the bed of my mistress was not, and never could be, Queen Helen of Sparta.

I ran away, though I could not possibly run fast enough. A familiar laugh trailed after me as I scampered back down the corridor. Not the queen's laugh. That sound was Chloris, through and through. Was it really the prince grunting beneath her, or had she wiped the prince's face over that of a bath slave as easily as Helen and Paris had wiped letters on and off the Phoenician papyrus?

*I know a few secrets,* Chloris had said. She was Phoenician herself, so she had always claimed. What other magics did she have?

I hurried my step, but her words caught up to my mind finally. *Break another pot.*

They wanted to be caught. Whether he was the real Paris or not, they were doing it in the name of that horrid prince. He was the only one who would benefit from Queen Helen's reputation being sullied in her husband's house. Did he expect her to seek refuge in his ships when King Menelaos lost faith in her?

Chloris, Chloris, what have you done?

Queen Helen was not in the main hall. I stared in horror at the Queen's empty seat. If only she had remained here, under her husband's eye, no man could ever accuse her. Perhaps there was still time...

But no, there was already a shouting from above, and I could see the king noting the commotion.

I turned and ran again, cursing the palace for its maze-like corridors. I fled to the east wing where the children slept and there, emerging from her daughter's bed chamber, was Queen Helen at last.

'My queen,' I gasped. 'Danger. You are accused...'

'Why,' said Helen with a half-smile across her beautiful face. 'Who accuses me? Have I committed some offence?'

'One of your servants — wears your face — in your bed, my queen. With Prince Paris....'

Helen's face went very still. Her smile faded into nothing. 'There is still hope, Hymnia,' she said after a moment's thought. 'Catch up the babies — no, wait. Let them sleep for now. I shall find my husband and show him my innocence.'

She took my hand, walking steadily, though I could see she was afraid of the outcry and bustle we could hear coming from the main part of the palace. Footsteps came running towards us, and Helen raised her voice to call the guards, only to realise that these armoured men were not hers to command.

Trojans wearing the false colours of Sparta advanced upon us, weapons at the ready.

'Come quietly, madam,' said one of them. 'We would hate to ruin that pretty face of yours.'

Helen shoved me suddenly towards them and I fell willingly, grasping at their blades in the hopes of taking them inside me, of saving my queen. Pain blurred through my body, and the last thing I saw was red and black and feathers.

~ઈ~

Not dead.

I was not dead, for I awoke again in the knowledge that I had failed. The ground swayed beneath me, back and forth, and bile rose in my mouth at the unnatural motion. I rolled over in the narrow bunk and opened my eyes.

A ship, then. I knew this ship. It was the same cabin I had visited so many times, to deliver those wretched messages back and forth on the magic papyrus. If only we had it now, perhaps we could summon help.

But who would listen to us, the captured queen and her slave?

Helen sat on a packing crate, barely glancing in my direction as I made my state known to her. 'All is lost,' she said softly. 'By now, my husband thinks me a madwoman, run away to sea in my lust for a Trojan sword.' She said those last few words with great distaste. Whatever she had once thought of Paris as they exchanged flirtation and banter, he was not beautiful to her now. 'I will never see my children again.'

She wept then, and I did not dare to comfort her. There was nothing I could say.

A Trojan sailor brought oils and fresh water to Helen, commanding her to make herself presentable for Prince Paris. My queen spat at him.

The sailor smirked at her, darting out of range with a nimbleness hardly suited to one who pulls ropes all day. 'A fine obedient bride my master has bought himself,' he chided her.

I knew then who this was. No sailor at all, not with that prissy manner and the secret smile he hid behind the insults. 'Chloris. Are you so ashamed of your real face now?'

The sailor gave me an arch look. 'My master thought it a sensible precaution if I was to live among his soldiers and sailors for a time. Women are unlucky at sea, you know. At the first sign of a storm, they'll be demanding he throw one or both of you overboard.'

'You're the one, then,' said Queen Helen in a low voice. 'The traitor who sold me to the Trojans.'

The sailor passed a hand over his face and became Chloris, as snub-nosed and freckled as I remembered her. 'I never served you, lady. I betrayed no one.'

'You betrayed me!' I said, outraged. 'You used me to get close to Prince Paris, and to wreck our lives.'

Chloris scoffed. 'How can I have betrayed you, Hymnia? You're not a real person. You're property, just as I was property. We don't have feelings, or loyalties. We are just owned.' She sneered at my queen. 'And now she is going to know exactly how that feels.'

Queen Helen leaped to her feet, striding towards the girl. Her golden hair tufted up like the feathers of an angry bird. 'You little snake,' she breathed. 'You have started a war, and orphaned my children, and for what? A prince who will never remember your name?'

'He knows my name,' Chloris growled at her. She passed her hand over her face again and became Helen, that Helen I had seen in my mistress's bed, the slightly too-perfect version of the golden queen. 'He calls me Helen, and Wife, and Queen, and Mine. He calls me Ohhh and Harder and Do That and Bend Over.' She preened at the queen whose face she had stolen. 'He's already had you, in every way possible, without ever laying a hand on your precious skin. You really should have listened when he said you belonged to him.'

The real Queen Helen hissed between her teeth. 'He still wants me, though, doesn't he? He wants the woman who said no, not the one who says "yes, master". He wants my ambrosia wrapped around his cock, not a pale imitation.'

Chloris frowned at that. 'I may be an imitation, lady, but if you don't submit to him fast enough, I'll be the one he carries home to Troy as a trophy. He told the whole city he was going to marry Helen of Sparta, and one way or another, he's going to be true.'

Helen's face became very calm, which always happened when she was dealing with someone very annoying, or very dull. 'Well, then,' she said. 'I had better hurry up and submit to my new husband, hadn't I? If nothing else, it will put you out of a job.'

～ℒ～

So he came to her, Prince Paris of Troy, the doom of queens. To summon him, Helen slapped Chloris across the face and scrawled the words 'I submit' across the girl's face in fiery words as magic as the ones that had once appeared and disappeared on the enchanted papyrus. Then she threw the girl out of the cabin, to be her messenger.

The prince arrived, stinking of oils and scent, delighted with himself. Chloris came too, clutching at her master's back, probably half-hoping that Helen had served the invitation in order to reject the prince.

But no, Helen was the Queen of Sparta and had been a wife for many years. She knew what to do with a man. She placed herself on the narrow bunk, the picture of docility, with her gown artfully arranged so that he would look at nothing but her breasts.

'Your highness,' she said in a voice that was neutral with only a hint of frost. 'I hear that we are to be wed.'

'Oh, my Helen,' breathed the lying prince. 'I would not take you against your will.'

She showed not even a flicker of distaste. 'If this is our destiny, then indeed we must be married. You have given me little choice but to obey.'

'Obey me in my arms, not with your mouth,' said Paris, flinging himself at her. 'Though I will have your mouth too.'

They sank back on to the bed, his mouth lapping at hers.

Chloris stood as a statue, leaning on the closed cabin door as the sea gently rocked us, and Paris groped beneath the gown of his new wife.

'You made this marriage,' I said in a low voice, gripping her wrist with my fingers, nails digging into her skin. 'The least you could do is witness it.'

There were cries coming from the bunk now, cries and groans, and I wanted to shut my ears to it, but I wanted more for Chloris to see what she had done.

Her face changed, though, and I saw fear on her face. Then I, too, looked towards the couple.

Paris struggled in the arms of Helen, and it was not pleasure that came out of his mouth now in those cries and groans. Her arms wound hard around his neck, and trails of white feathers burst from her skin from wrist to elbow, wet and spiky.

She rolled him over and straddled him effortlessly, letting her gown fall away as she did so and feathers, there were more white feathers everywhere, sliding from her shoulder blades in the long dipping shapes of wings.

Paris shuddered beneath her as her hands lengthened into golden claws and sank into his oily flesh.

'You have burned my life,' she told him, tipping back her head and letting her scalp burst into bright white feathers, streaked with blood. 'But I will eat yours.'

Chloris cried out, turning her face into my shoulder so as not to see Helen's face transformed into a streak of whiteness with a bright golden beak instead of a mouth.

Swift and bright as the sun, she pecked again and again, tearing at his skin, his flesh. Then she caught him up, divine creature that she was, and burst through the side of the ship. We rocked back and forth, water pouring in the damaged side, and Helen of Sparta flew free of us, still biting at the ruined body of the prince. Finally, high above the water and far enough from the ship that no one would ever rescue him, she dropped the creature like a stone.

We heard running and thumping from the sailors above us fighting to keep the craft afloat. My feet were wet. Helen was flying and flying, barely a dot on the horizon now. She was free, and she had left us long behind.

There was a pounding on the door behind us. Paris had barred it when he thought this was his wedding night, but now it was only a few splinters between us and a crew of sailors we did not know.

'Highness, Prince Paris!' cried out his men. 'We must leap to one of the other ships, we are sinking!'

Chloris and I, equally abandoned by our queen, stared at each other.

'They will tear us apart,' I whispered.

Chloris shook her head, and changed herself into the false Helen, the sprite she had worn for Prince Paris' benefit. 'Not me. I will be brought safely to Troy.'

'You fool,' I hissed. 'Do you think Menelaos won't start a war over this?'

'He will rescue me, then. I don't care. I just want to live. Not one of them ever thought I was worth keeping alive, not even your precious queen.' She pouted at me. 'If Paris is alive, Helen will be safe.'

'Paris is feeding the fishes now.'

'I know,' she said softly as the door shuddered behind us, again and again. They were trying to kick it in. 'I need another Paris, to keep me safe. To keep us both safe. I won't be a slave again.'

I closed my eyes, and felt Chloris' hand brush over me, transforming me with her Egyptian spells. 'It won't work, we can't be them,' I tried to convince her.

'We can be them more easily than they could ever be us,' she replied.

It was painless and drugging, the illusion she wrought upon me. When I looked into the polished bronze, though, I could not deny that it was convincing. The sight of myself made me tremble down to my toes.

When the sailors knocked down the door, they found Prince Paris of Troy and his new queen, Helen, waiting for rescue. Not once, as they pulled us along to alight from one ship and row to another in the fleet, not once did even a single sailor remember that Helen had been accompanied by a slave girl.

Hymnia had disappeared entirely.

I could not imagine my future, as we sailed onwards to Troy. This trick was not of my making, and yet I had agreed to it.

I was a Prince, and Chloris was a Queen. If there was a war now, we would be at the heart of it.

My heart broke for Helen, the real Helen, flying across the ocean in that monstrous form of beak and feathers. A mother without children, a wife without a husband, a Queen without a city.

And yet, as long as I had known her, she had never been more magnificent as when she caught up that wretched, sorry excuse for a prince and let him sink into the waters.

Whatever songs they sing of Helen — once of Sparta, now of Troy — whatever lies they tell, I shall always remember her as a swan, and flying, and free.

# THE MINOTAUR GIRLS

Only the hottest girls in town got picked for the Minotaur.

Like everyone else when I was fourteen, I wanted it desperately. I wanted to be like willowy Amber Sanders who was taken by the Minotaur the year before. Maybe I could dye my hair from mousy brown to fire engine red, and attain the mythical, miraculous status of *glitter*.

My mates and I weren't even glitter enough to get past the velvet rope. Thin Lizzie and Fat Lizzie and Chrissy and me, we tried a few Saturday nights, but it was humiliating to stand there in our best silver bubble-skirts and white tights, frizzed-high fringes and skates hanging around our neck, hoping that the door bitch would let us past.

We never even saw the door bitch. The lads on the door wouldn't let us past the first rope to get to her. We were too young, too wide-eyed, too daft.

So unglitter.

～ॐ～

We skated in the park instead, wobbling around the bike ramps and hoping not to ladder our tights. If we couldn't have the silver lights and pounding music of the Minotaur, at least we had this.

If we practiced and practiced, if we were hell on wheels, it wouldn't matter how we looked, right? The Minotaur would beg us to join them.

Sometimes Thin Lizzie's brother Sean and his bogan mates would join us, and sometimes they had beer. They didn't care that we were young — I think they liked trying to impress us. Eventually we paired off, for pashing and groping. This was practice too, I told myself, as I tried to keep Richie Mason's wandering hands from going too far past my bra.

A Minotaur girl had to be good at everything.

~ℒ~

One Monday, Fat Lizzie wasn't in class. The rumours were flying around the school by lunch. She had been seen, walking into the Minotaur in broad daylight. Wearing their uniform, the crisp white mini-dress, and brand new silver skates.

Our mate had been taken, and she hadn't even said goodbye.

'Why her, though?' said Chrissy as we ate dim sims at the corner shop after school. 'She's... well, you know.'

'Fat,' said Thin Lizzie, who wasn't especially thin.

We sat in quiet reflection of how horrible it must be to be slightly fatter than your friends.

'Must have been the boobs,' Chrissy decided, and we all agreed. Fat Lizzie filled a bra like no one else.

'Listen to us,' I said. 'Talking like she's dead. She's on the inside, isn't she? She's still our mate. Do you think she'd let us in one night?'

There was a long silence, as we thought about that.

'She won't want to know us now,' said Chrissy. 'No one ever comes back.'

~ℒ~

I practiced skating even harder. The Fat Lizzie thing gave me hope. It might be my turn next. So I went to the park even when the others couldn't be bothered, and I rolled and spun and did every trick that I could.

*Notice me, notice me, notice me.*

One evening, I spotted a boy watching me on the bike ramps. He had a nice shirt, all silvery, and when I stopped and matched his stare with my own, I recognised him.

He used to hang out with Thin Lizzie's brother Sean last year, before the boys started noticing us. I didn't remember his name, maybe Ade or Ollie. He'd gone missing a while back and everyone thought he shot through to the big city, looking for work.

It had never occurred to us that maybe the Minotaur took boys too.

They had made him beautiful. His hair was like frosted snow, and his eyes a bright jewel-blue that didn't exist in real life. He had the perfect jeans, fitted to his hips like they were sewn onto him. Glitter all the way.

He lounged on the edge of the ramp. And oh, he was watching me.

I did a flip and skidded up the slope to land near him, breathing harder than I wanted to. 'Hey.'

'You're good,' he said. His voice was beautiful too. It reminded me of expensive soap and Milli Vanilli.

'I practice a lot,' I said, and could have kicked myself. You're not supposed to show how much effort it takes to be good. You're supposed to be floaty and gorgeous and not even try. 'I mean, it's the best park for skating. I'm Tess.'

Did I sound desperate or what? I flopped down next to him, not looking at those beautiful bright eyes, pretending not to care that I sounded like a dropkick.

He didn't tell me his name.

'You're one of them,' I said. 'A Minotaur boy.'

He smiled softly. Sunlight gleamed on his hair. Glitter on a stick. 'Is that what you call us?'

'What do you call the rest of us?'

A gentle shrug. 'We don't think about you much at all.'

Anger burned through me. 'Say hello to Fat Lizzie for me. I used to be her friend.' I pushed myself up, rolling down the ramp, wanting to get away from him as fast as I could.

Something flashed in the air in front of me and bounced, ringing on the ramp. I skidded and leaned down to pick it up.

A silver coin with a Minotaur printed on it, and the words Admit One stamped on the back. I'd never seen one before, but older girls giggled about them sometimes, the tokens that get you past the velvet rope. Two prefects had once had a slap fight in the quadrangle over one they had found in the street.

The coin was warm in my hand. I looked up, shielding my eyes against the sun reflecting off the boy's frosted hair. For the first time in my life, I felt brave.

'I have two friends,' I said loudly. 'I go with them, or not at all.'

The Minotaur boy stared at me for a moment, and then he began to laugh.

~ꞗ~

Glitter is an attitude, not just a look. I had never felt as glitter as I did that day I showed Chrissy and Thin Lizzie what I had for us. Three perfect silver coins. Minotaur tokens.

'Unbelievable,' breathed Chrissy.

Thin Lizzie was frowning, turning hers over in her hand. 'What did you do for this, Tess?' she asked finally.

My cheeks went hot. 'I skated really well in the park, and he gave them to me.'

Thin Lizzie's eyebrows went up. I hated her in that moment. If she was going to be a mole, I didn't want her to have the coin at all.

Was this why Fat Lizzie never got in touch, when the Minotaur took her? Did she think we would be bitchy about it?

'You don't have to come,' I muttered.

Thin Lizzie smiled. 'Of course I'm coming.'

'This is so awesome,' Chrissy squealed. 'What are we going to wear?'

~ꞗ~

We touched our skates up with silver paint and shared a brand new frosted lipstick. My hand was hot from holding on to the coin all the way to the club. The lads on the rope let us through, and we found ourselves stumbling through a dark corridor towards the door bitch.

Her fringe was sprayed so high it almost brushed the top of the doorway. I'd never seen anyone with a nose stud before, and tried not to stare at it.

'You're the ones Ari invited,' she said, taking in our carefully assembled outfits. I waited for her to kick us out for being so unglitter.

Ari. His name was Ari.

The door bitch pulled back a dark curtain and the air was thick with music, a pounding beat that made my teeth hurt. Silver lights blazed out at us.

'Skates on, chickadees,' said the door bitch, and gave Thin Lizzie a push so she ended up in front of us, sliding on the polished floor. 'Ante up.'

We had made it to the Minotaur, and it hadn't cost us anything.

Skates on. Ante up.

~ॐ~

It was bigger inside than I had ever imagined. Ramps ran up the walls from room to room, and the lights dipped and spun from an impossibly high ceiling, making the shapes and the curves change every time. It was the best skating rink ever, times a million.

I lost Thin Lizzie. She was ahead of us, and plunged down a chute with some other girls, screaming and laughing. By the time Chrissy and I got there, Lizzie was nowhere in sight.

'We'll stick together, yeah, Tess?' Chrissy said, and I nodded reluctantly. The music was loud and amazing, with a beat that got inside my arms and legs. I didn't want her holding me back. I wanted to dance and skate and kiss boys and drink pink drinks and...

Chrissy seemed small.

We skated together, down a long channel into a high-ceilinged room where skaters flipped and tumbled their way up the walls, and a bright silver disco ball threw rainbow refractions against them. The ball spun, and the world shifted.

Sometimes when the light fell on them, they didn't look gorgeous at all. They looked like monsters. Their eyes glowed and their limbs undulated. Their sprayed hair became flowing lion manes, their lipsticked mouths became beaks, and there were snakes coiling everywhere, from their scalps to their pubes.

When the light shifted, they were beautiful again.

I still wanted to kiss them.

A tall monster with dreadlocked hair and kicky pink skates screeched up in front of me, grinning like a demon. I let her pull me into the maze of ramps. I did my best tricks and she laughed, clapping in delight. I spun and whirled, and if there were feathers flying from my arms now, I hardly noticed them.

I wasn't a monster or anything. Not yet.

Pink Skates tugged me into another room, and I lost Chrissy altogether. I didn't care. This one had a bright purple disco ball that cast grape-coloured shadows. The walls were soft and padded like the room was one big lounge suite. Someone gave me a drink and I gulped it gratefully before the sting hit the back of my throat and I realised that it wasn't water. It was like acid going down but then it warmed me up all over and I drank more of it.

No one was skating here, or if they were it was a long and lazy dance. Mostly they were pashing, limbs tangled together, heads tipped back against the soft parts of the walls, hands vanishing under layers of designer clothing.

I felt my face flame red with embarrassment. I don't know why. I hadn't cared at all that time Thin Lizzie and her first boyfriend started heavy petting in the park while the rest of us were right there, talking about which of the Coreys was cuter.

Some of these people were going further than heavy petting, but it was dark and the music was loud, and I didn't want to stare.

Kids were gaming in here too, with silver tokens like the ones

Ari had given me. Several beautiful Minotaur Girls leaned over a green baize table, flipping coins back and forth for the customers. I didn't understand the game.

I still wanted to play.

Pink Skates turned and kissed me. My head fell back against the cushiony padded walls. I was so light, my skates were the only thing holding me down. She tasted of raspberry lipgloss.

'Bet you can't guess my name,' she whispered.

Whoops and hollers awoke me from my daze. I pulled away from her, but no one was looking at us. The skaters and the gamers and the make-out artists all looked up, pointing and hooting at a boy in a cage that hung from the high ceiling, gleaming like a mirrorball.

'Go on,' Pink Skates said, more urgently. 'Bet.'

The boy was not laughing. He flinched as they threw bags of cellophane confetti which burst against the cage.

He was Ari, the silver boy who had given me the coins.

'What did he do?' I breathed. Why were they punishing him?

Pink Skates gave me an odd look. 'He won at the tables, and this is his prize,' she said. 'I'd love to be in the cage. Everyone looks at you. Guess my name, or you lose the bet.'

'Rose,' I said at random, the pinkest name I could think of.

'Wrong,' she laughed, and kept on laughing until she could barely breathe. 'I win!'

'What are you —' I started to say, and then something slammed into my chest. I gasped through the pain, falling to my knees. It hurt. My breasts were on fire from the inside out, and my stomach cramped like I was having five periods all at once.

Pink Skates did a pirouette in front of me, glowing with light and happiness. 'Standard ante,' she said. 'A year of your life. You should be more careful who you bet with, chickadee.'

'Why me?' I demanded of her. The pain began to ease, and I struggled to my feet.

'Why not? Baby dolls like you taste good. Fresh meat.' She skated away, still laughing.

This was the Minotaur. Music so loud it hurt, bored kids

causing pain for kicks and oh yes, being taunted in a glowing mirror ball cage was some kind of reward.

All I'd ever wanted to do was skate.

Somewhere in the dazzle and the brightness, I heard a scream. Was that Chrissy? I should never have left her alone.

I forced my way through several rooms of skaters and dancers and gaming tables and ramps, dazzling lights and dark shadows. Hands plucked at me, but I shook them off and kept going. 'Chrissy!'

I found her in a ball pit below a beautiful glass ramp that looked like something Cinderella would have skated down.

'These people are skanks,' Chrissy said breathlessly as I helped her climb out from under the writhing bodies. 'Some of the girls were kissing other girls!'

'Yeah,' I said uneasily. 'Let's get out of here.'

I had seen a big purple EXIT sign before, but I wasn't sure where.

'Going somewhere?' jeered a voice.

Thin Lizzie. She had come in here with us less than an hour ago, but I guess she'd made some new friends. She stood with them now, chewing gum and staring at me.

'I'm over this,' I said defiantly.

Thin Lizzie glided forward, daring me to push her or prove my uncool in some other way. 'They say I can stay if I stop you both leaving,' she said. 'I can come every night. Maybe earn my ticket into being a real Minotaur girl. Don't spoil this for me, Tess.'

'I want to go home,' Chrissy whined.

'You'd like it if you gave it a chance,' said Lizzie. 'Don't be such a chickenshit.'

I faced her down. 'If this place is so glitter, why are they trying to stop us leaving?'

But I knew that already. They didn't want me shouting my mouth off about how gross the Minotaur really was.

An older boy, with dark eyes and a smile I might have thought was charming about fifteen minutes ago, put his hand on Thin

Lizzie's shoulder. 'You can leave, babe,' he said to me. 'Anytime you want. But first you have to skate.'

~ℒ~

They took me to an arena deep in the Minotaur, with a plain round skating rink. A spotlight fell on me and I wondered for one laughable moment if this was some kind of reward, like it had been for Ari.

Teenagers leaned over balconies and sprawled across banks of velour seats.

The Minotaur girls stood at the edge of the rink, beautiful and silver and nearly identical. Never mind the spotlight, I was blinded by their pearly white eyeshadow. There were a few boys with them too, just as pretty.

My eyelashes prickled with sweat, and the audience took on other shapes before my eyes. Monsters all, teeth and claws. Laughing, sneering, glittering monsters.

I searched the crowd for one friendly face, but Chrissy stood with Thin Lizzie, their fingers entwined. She wasn't going to save me.

So I skated for the monsters. The lights grew brighter, and the music pounded in my ears only slightly louder than my heartbeat. I spun and whirled.

I could see the monsters more clearly now. Thin silver threads flowed from their wrists and ankles, spiralling upwards into the ceiling. Every time one of them moved or jerked a head, I saw a thread tug at them.

Even Chrissy had threads, though hers were paler than everyone else's.

I kept skating, pulling out every trick and flourish that I knew. A chime rang out above the music, and the Minotaur girls joined me on the rink, wheels flashing.

While I was skating, I was one of them.

I slowed, and immediately saw the difference. The Minotaur girls turned towards me with sneers and suspicion. I sped up, did a twirl or two, and they relaxed.

No way I could do this forever. My skates felt like concrete blocks on my feet.

Thin Lizzie and Chrissy skated together. They did not look at me. Thin Lizzie's threads were almost as bright as those of the real Minotaur girls, and Chrissy's glowed as she gained confidence.

If I stayed longer, I might not want to leave either.

A silver shadow poured from the ceiling to the floor. Everyone skated around it, pretending it wasn't there. It was a rope ladder, made of those threads they all wore. A silver ladder of knotted threads. It couldn't take my weight, surely?

But it was a chance.

I spun and danced and sped around the rink, not aiming for the ladder at all. I even let a Minotaur boy or two catch my hand and twirl me around. Non-threatening. Part of the show.

Then I skated backwards until I felt the soft brush of the thread ladder against my back.

I grabbed hold and climbed, pulling it up behind me. Up and up, and I hardly needed the ladder after a while because the silver threads were a thick tangle up here, twitching in the air. I climbed and climbed, and finally grasped something solid instead of that diaphanous ladder. It was a hanging cage. The knotted ladder ended here. I could see where the web of threads had been torn around us, to make the ladder.

'You,' said a whispered voice, and I saw the boy Ari staring out at me, his thin fingers grasping the bars. 'Is it you?'

He was so pathetic, my stomach swelled up with anger against him. 'Why did you give me that coin?' I hissed. 'Why did you bring me here? This place is horrible.'

Ari was still beautiful, but not nearly as glitter as he had seemed that day in the park. 'I didn't have a choice,' he said. 'The Minotaur made me do it. But I hoped… it might be different this time. Maybe you could break this place wide open. Someone has to.'

I hadn't thought of that. Could I close down the Minotaur once and for all? 'Everyone would hate me,' I said in awe at the very idea of it.

Ari smiled with bright teeth and yeah, I'd still let him kiss me. 'They'd never forget you,' he said.

~ℒ~

I broke two fingernails getting his cage open. I had to use a skate to bash at the lock until it broke and Ari could get out. We climbed together, up the chain that held the cage, and it wasn't long before we spotted a railing at the top of the Minotaur. There was a balcony running around the inside of this upper part of the building, and we clambered across the web of threads to reach it.

If we fell, we would be caught in those threads like the net under a trapeze. So many threads, each plugged into a beautiful monster.

Ari was right. We had to blow this place wide open.

'Where are we going?' I whispered.

'Control room,' Ari said back. 'There's always someone pulling the threads.'

'Like — a big boss?'

'I can't answer that,' he said, as I climbed over the railing. Finally, solid floor under my feet. He didn't once try to help me and I wasn't sure if that was wonderful or really annoying. 'A different girl pulls the threads each night.'

'How does all this happen without someone in charge?'

'It's the Minotaur,' said Ari. 'The building is alive. It wants us to have a good time and put on a show. It loves roller skates, who knows why. If we make it happy, it rewards us. So we do.'

We were outside the control room now. It had a wide glass window but I couldn't see much in the darkness.

Ari hung back.

'Aren't you coming in?' I asked.

'I don't think I can.' He lifted his feet and hands. Pale threads veined away from him and down over the edge of the balcony. 'They always grow back,' he said sadly.

I ran inside the control room and slammed the door behind me. 'So,' I said aloud. 'Who's pulling the threads tonight?'

'Tess?' said a small voice. 'Is that you?'

As my eyes got used to the darkness, I saw her at the far end of the room. She sat on an ordinary office chair, the kind that spins around. Every inch of her body had a silver thread growing out of it. They lashed into the walls and floor and ceiling.

Fat Lizzie. I hadn't seen her in weeks, but she looked different. Gaunt and angry and so, so scared.

'What have they done to you?' I breathed.

'It's not they,' she said. 'There isn't a "they". It's the Minotaur. She hates us all.'

The floor shuddered under my feet. The Minotaur didn't like us having this conversation. And since when was the Minotaur a she?

'What happens if I cut you out of those threads?' I asked Fat Lizzie.

'They grow back. Faster. And they hurt.'

I turned to the control banks, all those switches and dials. I pressed a button, and a screen flicked into life slowly, in greyscale. Another screen, then another. You could see the whole Minotaur from here, every room and ramp. The girls and boys were skating, gaming, kissing and groping.

'Not much of a show,' I said aloud. 'What if I make it more entertaining?'

The floor stopped rumbling under my feet. The Minotaur was curious.

'You can't beat the Minotaur, Tess,' said Fat Lizzie. She sounded stretched thin. 'She won't let you.'

That stung. Ari thought I was special. Why was she so certain I wasn't? 'Why not?'

Lizzie didn't answer. Her hands moved back and forth, plucking at the silvery threads that spun out through the walls and floors.

I left the control room and went back out to the balcony, where Ari lay trapped in his own tangle of silver threads. 'Why me?' I demanded. 'Why did you choose *me* if I'm so useless?'

He shook his head, staring up at me.

'Why am I the only one without silver threads sticking out of me?' I tried. This time, when he didn't answer, I flew at him, tearing at the threads. He yelled with pain as I pulled them out. When the last of them snaked away off the edge of the balcony, Ari sat there, breathless and rumpled but able to talk to me again.

'What are we going to do?' I demanded. I was no use on my own. I should be part of a group, with Lizzie and Lizzie and Chrissy bouncing our every word and thought off each other until everything made sense.

I missed them so badly.

'Don't ask me,' Ari snapped. 'This is your game, not mine. Don't you get it? You're the hero and I'm the fucking damsel in distress.'

Something rang a chord in my mind, so very familiar. 'What do you mean, game?'

'Ante-up, lay your bets, roll the dice,' he said in a sing-song voice. 'I laid my bets on you, Tess, and you're not exactly paying off.'

'Who am I playing against?' I hissed at him.

He glanced past me and shuddered. 'The Minotaur.'

I turned, not sure what to expect. My worst fear was that it would be one of my girls, Thin Lizzie or Chrissy, that I'd have to fight them. But it wasn't anyone I knew.

She wasn't tall. She was old like Mum, and I felt a familiar shock as I gazed at her, like meeting a long-lost aunt for the first time. She was fitter than my Mum, with better hair. She had a really great suit, all purple velvet and pale pink lace, like something Prince would wear.

'You were right the first time, Tess,' said the Minotaur. 'There is a boss.'

'I knew it,' I said sourly. 'No way a building is this mean all on its own.'

'That's not exactly true. I am the building, and the building is me — the Minotaur and her maze. Bet you can't guess my name.'

'I'm not falling for that again.'

'Fair enough.' She grinned at me, like she was my age. I wish I could remember where I'd seen her before. 'My name is Teresa Maree Holland. Or it was, before I became the Minotaur. So long ago.'

I felt small and stupid, and that made me angrier. 'That's my name.'

'Obviously.'

'You expect me to believe that... you're me?'

'No, sweetheart,' the Minotaur said, all patronising like the teachers at school. 'You're *me*.'

'That's not *true*,' I flung at her.

She smirked at me, and I knew that expression so well that it chilled my insides. I'd practiced it in the mirror before coming here tonight, so I'd look like the confident one instead of tagging after Thin Lizzie like I always do. 'The reason you don't have threads sticking out of you is because you are all thread, my darling. That's what I made you from. Time to come home, chickadee.'

The Minotaur reached out to me, and I felt something tug inside my stomach. It was true. I could feel how my whole body was made of threads, coiled tightly to make my limbs and blood and skin. If she pulled hard enough, I would dissolve into whorls of thread, spinning and dancing in the air. I wasn't real, I didn't mean anything, I was temporary...

'*No*.' I wrenched myself away. 'I'm not you. I don't care what game you're playing...'

'Aces high,' she said with a wink. 'But you're more of a two of hearts, really. A three at most. Naïve enough to let one of my girls win a year of your life, which I'm rather put out about. I had plans for that year.'

'I'm *me*,' I said, enraged. 'I'm Tess, I'm a real person.'

'I was like you once. More than once. So fresh faced. I mean, look at your adorable baby doll body. Life was so glitter back then. All I wanted to do was skate, and go with cute boys, and cruise with my friends. Look at me now — I'm living the dream.'

'Apart from being old,' I shot at her.

She looked triumphant. 'You don't think I went to all this trouble just to see a younger version of myself scampering about, do you? Look at you, my dear, all fire and outrage. Big fringe, short skirt. The power of youth. I made you, and now I'm taking you back, like I do every time. Every Minotaur does, when she grows old.'

Every time. This had happened before. The knowledge fell into my head like a brick. It wasn't just her, not just *this* Minotaur. Kids like me, all over the world, eaten and absorbed by desperate middle-aged wannabes like her. She smiled at me, like a real mother might, and I knew it was true. I knew a lot of things I couldn't know unless it was all true, and I was the next version of her.

The Minotaur didn't want to pull my body apart into threads of nothing. She wanted to climb inside it, steal it for her own. Where would I be? Would I be her? I couldn't imagine anything worse.

'You are — so — *unglitter*!' I howled at her.

She actually laughed, as if the word meant nothing.

I don't know what they were about, those other girls. I don't know how many of them — of me — trudged obediently to the slaughter, letting the Minotaur take them and reshape them and put herself inside their young bodies so she could do it all over again, and again, and again.

What did she do to them, to make them not want to fight for their life? I thought about my friends, and the last time I was truly happy, that day in the park when we were all together. I was ready to fight.

I was aware of every thread in this body of mine, every mote of skin and drop of blood. She had built me for one purpose, to be the next Minotaur. She wanted to rule this world of skates and dance music all over again, to control the silver threads, and so she must have built that power into me so it would be there when she stole my fourteen-year-old body. Fifteen-year-old. That was a hard one to get used to.

I could see it all, just as I felt her reaching out to me, into me, awakening that power so that it would bring her home.

And I snapped the threads. Every time she reached for me, I severed the connection. She frowned and tried again, but I beat her back. *My body, my threads. Mine for the keeping.*

Mine to destroy.

This time, when she came at me, I yanked every thread in the place. I felt Fat Lizzy in the control room, hanging on to the threads for dear life, and I begged her to trust me, to let her burden go. They slipped from her, every thread, and snaked towards me.

The woman who thought herself the Minotaur howled, trying physically to prevent the threads from reaching me, but her power was weak and every thread made me so, so strong.

I called to them, the Minotaur girls and boys, the teens who just wanted to skate and play games, the audience, my friends, even Ari. *Come to me, give me your power, share it all with me, and I will set you free. Ante up. Bet on me.*

Offered a choice between my older self and a teenage girl who looked much like them, they chose me.

The look on the Old Minotaur's face when she realised she had lost was awful. I felt kind of bad for her. But that didn't stop me setting those kids loose on her.

*You thought you were free of them, grown-ups with their rules and stupid lectures. But she was here all the time, telling you what to do.*

They didn't like that, the Minotaur kids. They climbed to us, up the webs of silver threads, hungry and desperate and furious. The happy fun place was lost, the music had stopped, and they remembered now that they had homes and families and lives that had been stolen from them. That they had been stolen from.

They ate her alive, the horde of beautiful silver children with shiny hair and totally glitter outfits. They tore her to pieces, and I let them do it.

Afterwards they looked at me, all docile and obedient, with the blood of my older self still staining their mouths, like they wanted me to be in charge. They thought I would be better than her, because I was young like them, and they did not know how to go on from here.

Would I be the one to give them back their eternal skate party, their games and glamour and mirror balls? Would I make it all better?

'We're going to burn it down,' I told them. 'It's going to be so glitter. The most glitter ever. And after that, you can go home.'

The Minotaur burned, and the fire engines came, and there was nothing much left after that except charcoal and crying teenagers. I found my skates in the sparkling rubble.

'You did it,' Ari said to me. 'You broke the spell.'

'Yay for me,' I said flatly.

The parents came, one by one, to drive their kids home. Thin Lizzie's mum cried when she saw her. Chrissy's dad looked really fierce. Fat Lizzie's parents just looked relieved.

Ari and I waited, until they had all gone home, and it was just us.

I hadn't expected anyone to come for me. That mum and dad I thought I had, when we talked about our parents at school, or in the park... if they had ever existed, they belonged to the original Tess, generations ago. Gone now.

I didn't ask why no one had come for Ari. He didn't seem surprised.

'What now?' he asked.

My charred skates still had silver paint on them. 'Let's go to the park,' I said.

'And do what?' he said in disbelief. 'Skate? After all this?'

'It's the best park for skating.'

I knotted my laces together, hung my skates around my neck, and took his hand. We would skate a bit, and talk, and maybe kiss for a while. We would fall asleep on the cold grass of the park. And I would leave him there, before it got light. Where I was going next, I couldn't take him.

There were other Minotaurs in the world, in other towns. I knew that now, and I knew how to stop them. I had to locate the girls that were just like me, help them unravel the truth and the power within their own skin.

Skates on.

Ante up.

One thread at a time.

# SOME CUPIDS KILL WITH ARROWS

Meg should have known. This was what came of trying to be nice.

'It's a new job, a new crowd,' her mother had declared, far too cheerfully. 'Be sociable this time around. Make friends. Say yes to possibilities.'

Against her better judgement, Meg had worn the daffodil yellow shirt; Meg had said 'yes' to drinks after work with her bubbly deskmate Dee; Meg had allowed the dangerous overtures of friendship to wash over her like a fog of latte foam and borrowed lip gloss.

This was how Meg found herself here, at a speed-dating night in a pub called *Dog and Biscuit*, opposite a man who introduced himself as Hercules.

Hercules. Without a trace of irony.

Worse than that, this beefcake with a side of cheese would not stop banging on about his ex-wife. Whose name, apparently, Meg shared. Whose fate he kept alluding to as 'tragic.'

She knew what was going on here, and she was having none of it.

'So, you must be Hermes,' she accused the next man along the table, another Hollywood-gorgeous slab of everything with white teeth and sculpted muscle, though this one was spiky blond, and ran on sleeker lines than the mighty Hercules.

'Cupid,' said the blond, his forehead creasing slightly. 'Why did you think I was Hermes?'

'Wings on your shoes. Cupid would have been my next guess — or Eros. I wasn't sure if we were including Romans in the mix with the Ancient Greeks.'

'You figured us out fast,' he said, impressed.

'I have a Masters in Comparative Mythology. My mother said it would do nothing to prepare me for real life situations — ha, thanks for that. I think I just won a decades-old argument.'

'You intrigue me,' said Cupid, leaning in. 'What did you say your name was?'

Meg wore a name tag and was about to say something cutting about his failure to notice that, but it occurred to her that the reason he couldn't read her name tag was because he was gazing into her eyes as if he might find the secrets of the universe there — or possibly a really amazing fuck against a wall.

Either way, he wasn't looking at her name tag.

The bell rang, and Cupid released his intense scrutiny. As she moved on down the line, Meg felt like she was leaving half her clothes behind.

Theseus had a good run of chat up lines, and filled out a designer suit in interesting ways, but admitted within the first two minutes that his main goal in life was to have a threesome with a pair of sisters.

Jason talked about boats. Meg considered raising the question of *his* ex, to scope out the nature of his tragic backstory, but decided she did not want to know if this modern, gel-haired, soccer playing version of the ancient hero had once commanded his wife and children to be stoned to death.

～ߦ～

Finally, it was over, and she crawled to the bar — an oasis in a desert full of terrible men who didn't deserve her. 'I blame you,' she told Cupid, who had been sitting there for a while in his battered blue jeans and tight white t-shirt.

'Most people do,' he said, not taking offense. 'Can I buy you a —'

'Gin martini, dirty, followed by an immediate sequel,' she demanded. Letting men finish their sentences was overrated. That was the life lesson she was taking away from speed dating night.

'The preoccupation humanity has with romantic love is not my fault,' Cupid insisted, after he had ordered the drinks. 'You're the ones who chase after it like it's the boss level of a computer game.'

'Easy for you to say, you're married.' Meg had written her final thesis on Psyche and her magical fairytale of an invisible prince, of the mountains of seeds and the power of love.

'We broke up,' Cupid said morosely. He took the arrival of their drinks as a good excuse to throw back the rest of the beer he already had. 'Centuries back.'

Meg gave him a sharp look. 'Oh by all means, *let's* talk about your wife. I can't tell you how much my belief in Happy Ever After has been bolstered by tonight's parade of sad saps with their tales of marital woe.'

'She said I wasn't present enough in the relationship.'

'Was that a joke? Because of the invisibility thing when you first got together?'

'Might have been,' he sighed wistfully. 'Psyche had a knack for puns. And crossword puzzles. She was perfect.'

'Give me strength.' Meg looked around for Dee, only to see her bubbly blonde deskmate leaving on the arm of Hercules. 'Ugh.'

'Another drink?'

'It's the least that you owe me.'

Another half martini later, Cupid said in a plaintive voice, 'Didn't you like any of them?'

'I knew it!' Meg said savagely. 'This whole night was for my benefit, wasn't it? You're on the clock, cupiding me. Not that "cupid" should ever be a verb. Why on earth would you —' A horrible thought struck her. 'Am I one of you? I'm not Aphrodite, am I?'

'No,' said Cupid with a special kind of horror in his voice. 'You are not my mother. I think I would have noticed.'

'Are we related?'

'There's no Greek god in you, I promise.' There was a long pause as if they were both listening to the obvious follow-up line to that: *Would you like one?*

'Thank fuck for that.' Meg chewed on an olive. 'So why am I special enough to warrant my own magical mystery speed dating session? And, more importantly, why pick *those* men?'

'Well,' said Cupid. 'You do have a Masters in Comparative Mythology. And you like muscles, according to your online profile and every Tumblr site you've ever visited.'

Ten out of ten for creepy stalker technique. 'And these are the only men you know,' she guessed.

'And these,' Cupid conceded. 'Are the only men I know. What was wrong with Ares?'

'Oh, do let's speculate about why *your father* the God of War might be an inappropriate romantic match for a highly sarcastic pacifist.' Meg blew out an exasperated breath. 'I can't tell you how much I'm looking forward to telling my mother about this evening. Impractical field of study my arse.'

Cupid looked as disappointed and pathetic as was possible for a man that handsome.

Meg elbowed him in a friendly manner. 'Why are you so terrible at this?'

'I think I forgot how to cupid. It's been a few centuries since I made the effort.'

'What have you been doing with yourself to get so rusty?'

'Your lot invented the novel. It distracted me.'

'Which novel in particular?'

'All of them. I'm still trying to catch up. I've got as far as 1965.'

'Oh, hang in there, you're nearly at *Valley of the Dolls*.'

'I just — I have to make a love connection between two people. This week.'

'That's specific.'

'My mother gave me an ultimatum. A century ago. To return to the family business, or lose everything.'

'And it slipped your mind until now?'

'Do you know how many novels were published in the 20th century? I was *busy*! A century goes by way too fast. I blame automobiles and the Internet. And Evelyn Waugh. Mostly Evelyn Waugh.'

This banter was the most fun Meg had made all night. 'You made one love connection,' she pointed out. 'Dee and Hercules looked very cozy as they left.'

'That's not love,' Cupid muttered. 'That's sex. They'll have three amazing weeks together, and then he'll cheat on her with one of his exes and she'll end up having a public meltdown in the office, throwing her phone out of a window, and causing a fatal accident to a pedestrian below. Which is actually better than what happened with the last three women he hooked up with.'

Meg stared at him for what felt like a very long minute. 'You can see those consequences, and you didn't stop them leaving together? Someone's going to *die*.'

'I can't stop humans making terrible choices when sex is on the line. Also, Hercules is excellent in bed. Apparently. I wouldn't know from personal experience.' Cupid looked shifty.

Meg had made a decision. It felt better than any other decision she had made all year. 'Come with me,' she said, catching hold of the strap of her handbag. 'We're going to go split those two up, and then we're going to find some nice ordinary non-disastrous couple for you to match, to keep your mother happy. In return, you are going to stay the hell away from my love life for the next, oh I don't know, century.'

Cupid stood up, swaying slightly, which made sense since he had drunk three martinis for every one of hers. 'You're wonderful,' he said. 'Are you sure you don't want me to cupid you? There's bound to be at least one gym bunny in this city who finds sarcasm a turn-on.'

Meg had a momentary vision of what Cupid might possibly look like under the very tight t-shirt. 'I'm good,' she said firmly. 'Let's go.'

'I don't know what the big deal is,' muttered Hercules later that evening, nursing a beer and a black eye in that order. 'I didn't cheat on you yet.'

'Three weeks!' said Dee huffily. 'You couldn't be monogamous for a *month*?'

'A theoretical three weeks! You don't know that would have happened. Cupid's full of shit.'

Dee turned her baby blues on Cupid. 'Are you full of shit?'

'Nope,' he said brightly. Meg thought he seemed remarkably cheerful about separating a couple instead of hooking them up. Perhaps this was the start of a new career for him? 'Love stinks, but I always tell the truth about it.'

'So who is my real future husband?' Dee asked, leaning in and fluttering her lashes. 'Is he cute?'

'No idea,' said Cupid, soaking up the blatant flirtation. 'We changed the future tonight. It will take a while for fate to catch up.' He lowered his voice intimately. 'Tonight, anything is possible.'

Meg found herself grinding her teeth every time Dee touched Cupid's hand. Oh, hell no.

'Full. Of. Shit,' Hercules mouthed at her, over Cupid and Dee's heads.

'You know what your problem is?' Meg said to Cupid.

He laid his head on the bar and sighed, but at least he was sighing in her direction again. 'My friends are the worst,' he complained.

'Your friends are the *worst*,' she agreed, and patted his head. His hair was very soft under her fingertips.

'Hey, I am sitting right here,' said Hercules.

'Assuming that Dee hasn't been entirely put off dating by tonight's mess,' Meg went on. 'Who is your least-worst friend?'

Cupid thought about it seriously. 'Odysseus is solid. And he could do with a pick-me-up since that whole Circe-Penelope mess. Though I have to admit, they are way cuter together than in that timeline where they both ended up dating each other's sons. You couldn't make this shit up.'

'I'm in, if this Odysseus isn't a complete cheating jerkwad,' Dee volunteered. She had reined in the Cupid-flirting, almost as if she sensed Meg's feelings and was being a good friend. Huh.

'Well,' considered Cupid. 'Not since the late 1700's.'

'Good enough for me,' said Dee.

'We can double date,' Meg decided.

Cupid gave her a searing look that made her shiver all the way down to her toes. 'Really?'

'Sure,' she said, though it was hard to pretend to be casual when you had All That zeroing in on you. 'I want to see how it turns out. Plus, you talk a good game about love and romance. Show me what you've got.'

Cupid's bright green eyes lit up. 'I will spoil you so thoroughly with romance, the sky itself will be jealous.'

Meg forgot to breathe for a moment.

'You are literally texting your ex right now,' Dee complained loudly. 'This is why no one wants to date you.'

'What?' Hercules shot back. 'I'm bored and no one is making out with me. Seems like a waste.'

'...And so we have plans tonight,' Meg completed in triumph.

Her mother, looking weary, removed her glasses and then put them on again. 'With this Cupid person.'

'Not this person. Actual Cupid! Which I know because of my...'

'Remarkably useful Comparative Mythology degree, yes, dear. I do take your point.'

'It's amazing how deftly you acknowledge I was right without actually saying the words,' Meg complained.

Her mother let out a deep sigh. 'Did it ever occur to you, my darling, that I might have had *other* reasons for preferring you to stay ignorant of certain mythological realities?'

Meg's mouthful of tea went cold instantly, and she spat it back into her cup. 'Excuse me, now?'

'A little knowledge can be very dangerous.'

'Oh god,' Meg moaned. 'Literally oh god. You're one of them. I knew this would happen. Are you Aphrodite? Did I spend an hour last night with my tongue down the throat of my son?'

'Please, that wench wishes she was me,' snapped her mother. 'We're not connected to that trashy Greek soap opera.'

'What about the Romans?' Meg wasn't sure if Cupid counted as Roman, Greek or both, and what even was her life, that this was of practical concern?

'We're not the toga brigade, either. Oh dear. I suppose you had to find out sooner or later...'

～ઈ～

'...And that's how I found out that my parents are Isis and Osiris,' Meg summed up. 'Have you seen the list of things that Isis is goddess of? Health, marriage, magic, the dead, oh and *wisdom*. So that's me giving up on winning an argument with her ever again. It was nice while it lasted.'

'You know,' said Cupid. 'It's amazing how few women keep talking about their mother when I've removed this many clothes. My mother, yes, no one ever shuts up about my mother during sex, I'm used to that, it's all "Venus in heaven!" this and "By Aphrodite's toes!" that, but I draw the line at other people's mothers.'

'I'm sorry,' said Meg. 'Was I not giving you enough attention? Is my major life crisis interrupting your boner?'

'Fine,' said Cupid, and took his hand out of her knickers. 'Mood officially lost, we'll come back to that later. Meg, believe me, this is not a life crisis. Having gods for parents is no big deal.'

'I thought they were librarians,' she wailed.

'They probably are librarians. God business doesn't pay that well in the 21st century. Now, do you want me to go down on you before we endure this double date from hell or not?'

'Why is it going to be a double date from hell?' Meg asked suspiciously. 'You said Odysseus and Dee would be great together.'

Cupid gave a small moan of frustration and put his t-shirt back on. 'Because,' he said, leaning across couch to kiss her lightly on the cheek. 'I'm not all that interested in spending the evening watching *people who are not us* flirt and connect, when we've got all this going on right here. Hence. Hell.'

'Oh,' said Meg, kissing him back. 'You really are —' kiss '— a half-hearted —' kiss '— love god.'

'Yeah,' said Cupid. 'But my tongue is in the right place.'

Before she could say 'Don't you mean heart?' he demonstrated quite thoroughly that he meant exactly what he said.

# SIX RECIPES USING POMEGRANATE SEEDS

## 1. CRUSHED DESIRE: A COCKTAIL

*Contains: pomegranate seeds and syrup. Champagne. Gin. Crushed ice.*

Smash as much ice as you can fit in the glass. Pour the sticky syrup over the ice, red and sweet.

Liberally scatter your wet red seeds from the freshly scooped pomegranate.

Cover with a pour of gin and top with champagne until the fizz bleeds pink.

Sip in public, slowly, until you catch the eye of the king of the underworld, who is seeking a bride. He will take care of the rest.

This is not a good recipe.

This is not a romance.

## 2. DIS MESS

*Contains: your cereal of choice, fresh milk, half a pomegranate.*

Make the cereal to taste. Hold the cut pomegranate upside down over your bowl and hit it with a heavy spoon until all the clotted seeds fall out. Stir into your cereal. Eat.

Yes, it's a little bitter.

Call your mother, and tell her where you are.

## 3. PATIENCE ON A PLATTER

*Contains: Milk, eggs, plain flour, salt, creme fraiche or cream cheese, pomegranates.*

Make your favourite basic pancake recipe, in miniature.

Top each pancake with a dollop of something creamy, and a healthy spoonful of pomegranate seeds.

Serve on a platter at the negotiating table, as the man who stole you debates with your mother about how many months you must spend living as his queen and wife, in the underworld.

Make more than you think you will need; the conversation will be lengthy and complicated.

## 4. NOURISHMENT

*Contains: the rind of 1 pomegranate, the stones of 3 apricots, the cores of four apples.*

Wash the ingredients in water from a mountain stream, then throw them away.

Drink the water. It's important to stay hydrated when all else seems lost.

## 5. SURF AND TURF AND DEAD

*Contains: one steak, six prawns and half a pomegranate per person.*

Marinate proteins in the dripped juices of the pomegranate. Grill on a barbecue until lightly blackened.

Garnish with black pepper and the ashes of the dead, to taste.

Grill it all over again.

Eat every bite. You need more than pomegranates to sustain you over the long winter.

## 6. SPRING COMPOTE

Break your last pomegranate open with your bare hands.

Warm the seeds slightly in the sunshine.

Eat in the fresh air, alone and free of the underworld. (For now.)

Savour.

~ʊ~

*This week's recipes were provided by Persephone. We hope she's doing okay.*

*Next week: Poseidon's top tips for a fisherman's basket.*

# WONDER WOMEN OF THE
# MYTHIC MULTIVERSE
## (AN AFTERWORD)

My favourite thing about Greek mythology — all mythology, though Greek was my first love — is that there is no canon. No true, correct, accepted version of any story.

Even our earliest extant versions of many myths contradict each other. They are supposed to exist as part of a single, colossal shared story, like the Marvel Cinematic Universe, but the stories all overlap and contradict each other, not by error but by design, like the larger Marvel multiverse.

Authored by everyone; owned by none. There was no copyright in the ancient world. We don't even know if Homer, one of the most famous western storytellers of all time, was a single person or a joyous collective of bards who really liked describing Dawn as 'rosy-fingered.'

This is particularly important when it comes to the women of Greek mythology, because if you stick to the same old authors and their versions of events, it gets depressing pretty quickly. Do you want to know that, after *The Iliad* ended, the women of the conquered Troy were all rounded up and handed out like party bags to the Greek generals? That Helen returned to her husband, and spends *The Odyssey* mixing various concoctions of drugs to forget her misery? That Medea murdered her children to wound her husband? That Theseus dumped Ariadne on an island and married her sister?

These versions of the stories aren't pretty. But they're also not the only ones out there. For as long as Greek mythology has existed — and long before the writing-down of the versions we have — playwrights and poets have been messing with the narrative, shaping their own versions of events. While Euripides did not invent the coffee shop AU or other modern fandom tropes, he did take a break from writing tragedies to pen a romantic comedy based on the idea that Helen never made it to Troy, but hung out in Egypt while the Trojan War was going on, and was finally reunited with her original husband in spite of the best efforts of the gods.

I still remember getting to the end of Kerry Greenwood's glorious novel *Medea* (1997, recently reprinted by ClanDestine Press) and being stunned that (spoilers) Medea does not kill her children. The novel concluded with an essay by Greenwood, referring to different versions of the story, including one urban legend that Euripides was paid by the city of Corinth to make Medea the scapegoat for the crime of their citizens.

Myth is not history. You can be devastated by the dark tragedy of Euripides' *Medea* and still hold Kerry Greenwood's novel in your heart.

It's possible that a grounding in Greek myth was a reason why I took so much enjoyment from the messy, sprawling shared universes of superheroes as a teenager — and later, when I discovered fanfic, how much fun I had reading completely different versions of the same story, over and over again.

~ও~

Then, along came Xena.

Falling in love with this show in the late 90s was a complex torment. I adored it, but tracking down episodes across the wild west of Australian broadcasting was an exercise in madness and creativity. The episodes were never shown in any predictable order, and in the days of early and unreliable internet, keeping track of what I'd missed was almost as hard as trying to understand the backstory of the X-Men in the days before Wikipedia.

While the emotional arcs of the show mostly made sense when watched in the correct order, the mythic 'history' did not. The philosophy behind *Hercules: The Legendary Journeys*, and its mostly superior sequel *Xena: Warrior Princess* was literally 'everything BC is good.'

An episode about the fall of Troy aired the week after an episode in which Spartacus' revolt was narrated. My brain sputtered and protested... and then went very quiet, as I took a deep breath and accepted that this was it. This was the show. There's no power in 'well, *actually*' here.

Everything BC is good.

Part of the reason that the *Xena* show was so much better than its *Hercules* predecessor, despite sharing creators, resources, a fictional universe, and the same fifteen New Zealand actors in various wigs, is that while *Hercules* brought humour and modern dialogue to the classic myths, it also attempted to map the modern Hollywood 'hero' archetype on to the ancient world. Which is a tricky proposition considering that ancient heroes are mostly assholes.

*Xena* interrogated the idea of 'hero' right from the start. A redeemed villain doing her best to make up for a dark past, while travelling alongside a naïve young bard who gradually has all her romantic assumptions about heroes stripped away.... This was a show that deconstructed myths in more ways than one.

The thing about myths is, **they start out deconstructed**. It's the attempts to assemble them into coherent timelines, tidy family trees or 'factual' histories that is doomed to failure.

-ᲒᲔ᠆

One of the most important things to know about the heroes of Greek myth is that they're the worst. In the 21st century, we think the word 'hero' means Superman, or Wonder Woman. A fire fighter during 9/11. A nurse during the pandemic.

In the ancient world, a hero was someone who did big things.

Epic things. Rarely good things. The deeper you get into the source material, it's hard to avoid how much of Greek mythology is about beautiful, extraordinary, interesting women having terrible things done to them by men, whether those men are mortals, heroes or gods.

Take Zeus, for example, the greatest and most powerful god of the Greek pantheon. King of the world. I could tell you about all the women he raped, and how many lives were destroyed because he couldn't keep it in his pants, but I would be here literally all day. His wife Hera was just as bad, regularly maiming, transforming or murdering women just because her husband had chosen to rape or harass them.

So many women of the ancient world had to put up with being 'captured', 'pursued', 'stolen', 'loved' against their will, often treated like game tokens to be presented at the end of a quest as a reward. Once you wade through the historical romanticisation of many of those encounters, it adds up to a whole lot of non-consensual activity.

What's really fascinating is that while we have very few extant works of the ancient world known to be written by women, the male authors themselves were often willing to challenge the idea that the only role of mythic women was to be wife, mother or trophy.

In Aeschylus' *Agamemnon*, his wife Queen Clytemnestra murders the king upon his return to Troy, in vengeance for his sacrifice of their daughter Iphigenia ten years previously. Other versions of the story soften her involvement, suggesting she manipulated her boyfriend Aegisthus into doing the crime, or that her main motive was lust for the new man, not justified fury at her husband's unforgivable deed. But in Aeschylus' play, Clytemnestra wields the axe herself, and makes it very clear she feels justified.

Then there's Ovid, a Roman poet whose work is full of all kinds of problematic content... but who also devoted an entire book to imaginary letters from the long-suffering women of ancient myth, addressed to their disappointing husbands and lovers. *Heroides* was one of the more eye-opening texts I discovered at university, as it was so extraordinary to see the mythic women of so many famous stories given their 'own' voice.

When I first started to write my own stories based on Greek myth, it was these angry wives of *Heroides* that I always returned to. Helen and Clytemnestra, sisters and queens both wrecked by the patriarchy. Demeter and Persephone, mother and daughter separated every year because Hades chose to steal a wife instead of courting her. Ariadne, ditched by Theseus. Deianeira, abandoned wife of Hercules. Medea, devastated and betrayed by Jason.

There are other women of the ancient world, however, and I found them all over again when writing my stories. Some of them don't even get raped or murdered! Atalanta, the only female Argonaut. Psyche, the original fairy tale heroine. Circe, my favourite enchantress.

Medusa, always Medusa. The woman who was made a monster as punishment for her own rape; a classic mythic trope if ever there was one. It's been delightful and fascinating in recent years to see Medusa reclaimed, the idea of a gorgon transformed into a powerful feminist figure in new art and stories. She deserves nice things.

Greek myth, that glorious and weird and horrible and powerful shared universe, is still open for business. We're still adding new stories, and re-shaping the old ones to suit ourselves.

~ક~

One of my favourite developments of ancient scholarship in the nearly-two-decades since I moved away from academia is the rise of female translators of Ancient Greek and Latin. When I was studying, there were plenty of wonderful female scholars, but only a handful of commercially-available translations of the classical works were translated by women. I am so excited now to be reintroduced to the worlds of Aeschylus, Sappho, Homer and Vergil via the translations of Anne Carson, Emily Wilson, Sarah Ruden and more. Finding new translators is my happy place.

Fresh translations are just as important, if not more so, as the wealth of re-imaginings and re-tellings. There's no such thing as a perfect translation any more than there is an exact, canonically accurate version of a myth. Even the oldest versions of these stories that we have may not be exactly what you thought they were, filtered through the voice and world view of a 1950s don, or an 18th century poet... these 21st century translations will age, too, and appear old fashioned one day, but they'll remain an essential piece of the puzzle.

Humans have been taking liberties with myth, and asking 'what if' since those stories first began to be told.

What if Helen never made it to Troy?

What if Clytemnestra had every right to be angry?

What if Medusa was not actually a monster...

What if they all teamed up to fight injustice?

What if they didn't have to?

# ABOUT THE AUTHOR

Tansy Rayner Roberts is an award winning blogger, podcaster and fantasy author who lives in Tasmania with her family. She has a PhD in Classics and a particular attachment to Roman history, which infuses her work.

Tansy's books range from the light-hearted SFF like Tea and Sympathetic Magic and Musketeer Space to the darker and more epic Creature Court. She also writes cozy murder mysteries under the name Livia Day. Tansy is one of the co-hosts of the popular Verity! podcast, discussing Doctor Who with women around the world.

In 2013, Tansy won the Hugo for Best Fan Writer thanks to the critical writing on her blog. This made her the first Australian woman ever to win a Hugo Award. She won it a second time in 2015 in the Best Fancast category with Galactic Suburbia.

Subscribe to her newsletter at tinyurl.com/tansyrr.

facebook.com/tansyrroberts

twitter.com/tansyrr

instagram.com/tansyrr

goodreads.com/tansyrr

patreon.com/tansyrr

# CREDITS

# THANK YOU FOR BUYING THIS BRAIN JAR PRESS CHAPBOOK

To receive special offers, bonus content, and info on new releases and other great reads, visit us online at www.BrainJarPress.com

CPSIA information can be obtained
at www.ICGtesting.com
Printed in the USA
BVHW081053080323
659899BV00007B/697